GREEN TO GREY

An Environmental Anthology

ESSENTIAL ANTHOLOGIES SERIES 17

Canada

ONTARIO ARTS COUNCIL
CONSEIL DES ARTS DE L'ONTARIO
an Ontario government agency
un organisme du gouvernement de l'Ontario

Canada Council for the Arts
Conseil des Arts du Canada

Guernica Editions Inc. acknowledges the support of the Canada Council for the Arts and the Ontario Arts Council. The Ontario Arts Council is an agency of the Government of Ontario.
We acknowledge the financial support of the Government of Canada.

GREEN TO GREY

An Environmental Anthology

edited by
Ian Thomas Shaw and Timothy Niedermann

GUERNICA EDITIONS

Toronto · Chicago · Buffalo · Lancaster (U.K.)
2025

Michael Mirolla & Connie McParland, general editors
Ian Thomas Shaw & Timothy Niedermann, editors
Cover and interior design: Ian Thomas Shaw

Guernica Editions Inc.
287 Templemead Drive, Hamilton (ON) L8W 2W4
2250 Military Road, Tonawanda, N.Y. 14150
www.guernicaeditions.com

Distributors:
Independent Publishers Group (IPG)
600 North Pulaski Road, Chicago IL 60624
University of Toronto Press Distribution (UTP)
5201 Dufferin Street, Toronto (ON) M3H 5T8

First edition.
Printed in Canada.

Legal Deposit—First Quarter
Library of Congress Catalog Card Number: 2023946407
Library and Archives Canada Cataloguing in Publication
Title: Green to grey : an environmental anthology / edited by Ian Thomas Shaw and Timothy Niedermann.
Names: Shaw, Ian Thomas, 1955- editor. | Niedermann, Timothy, 1953- editor.
Series: Essential anthologies series ; 17.
Description: First edition. | Series statement: Essential anthologies ; 17
Identifiers: Canadiana (print) 20230549020 | Canadiana (ebook) 20230549039 | ISBN 9781771839297 (softcover) | ISBN 9781771839303 (EPUB)
Subjects: LCSH: Climatic changes—Fiction. | LCSH: Environmental degradation —Fiction. | LCSH:
Environmentalism—Fiction. | CSH: Short stories, Canadian (English) | LCSH: Short stories, Canadian. | LCGFT: Short stories.
Classification: LCC PS8323.C6 G74 2025 | DDC C813/.010836—dc23

INTRODUCTION

The eclectic stories in this anthology speak to our changing climate and degrading environment—the transformation of our world from *green* to *grey*. Some stories are sardonic, treating environmental icons and self-serving rhetoricians equally. Others are whimsical, even bitterly so, and some are sweetly poetic. But their messages are the same: it is time to act.

Two stories by Ian Thomas Shaw, “Green-ish” and “Grey-ish,” bookend the anthology. These take pointed jabs at the current political inattention to the environment and how things might look fifty years in the future. Two immigrant stories take the collection into the nostalgic: Caroline Vu’s “Endangered Species” and Sang Kim’s “Wild Geese.” Vu, drawing on the fates of twin sisters, reminds us of the devastating effects of Agent Orange in Vietnam. Kim juxtaposes dwindling fish stocks and industrial pollution with a Korean-Canadian father’s failed attempt to secure his family’s love and respect. Rejection of middle-class values, personal disillusionment and the quest to make a difference on a societal level are explored in Jerry Levy’s “The Anarchist.” Nurture and nature are examined in Tim Niedermann’s “Green Toe,” a jab at the much-touted values of owning, controlling and shaping the natural world around us. Then, in “Trash Day,” Niedermann depicts the limits of middle-class environmental micro-activism against the enormity of consumerist pollution. Cora Siré’s “Patagonia” and Matt Murphy’s “Tio” take us to Latin America, where Siré offers a triptych view of environmental degradation in her beloved Patagonia, and Murphy juxtaposes the privilege of young Western tourists with the short, brutish lives of Bolivian miners.

From the green of the present, we enter the grey of the future. The protagonist of Ursula Pflug’s “Found Divination” laments the loss of starlight, both physically and spiritually. Michael Mirolla’s

“Hothouse Love,” a cautionary tale told to aliens, tells of the extinction of the destructively ubiquitous species we call humanity. Siré and Pflug then continue the theme of human loss in collapsed societies in their stories “Saving Morro” and “A Green and Just Recovery.”

If fiction is to serve a purpose, it should be to stimulate reflection on what we have done and are doing. As our world rolls toward the abyss of environmental collapse, can we not change course? Must we neglect the world around us as we grapple with our inner struggles and materialistic needs? We invite you, our readers, to decide.

— *The Editors*

Table of Contents

Green

GREEN-ISH

Ian Thomas Shaw

Another tornado warning? WTF! I look out the window at a sky filled with smoke from the forest fires in northern Quebec. Outside, the air has become deadly for anyone with asthma. Luckily my lungs are fine, and I had been thinking of putting on a mask and going for a bike ride despite the smoke, but a tornado is something else.

My God, just two months ago the Ottawa River was flooding homes in the area. Now we are plagued by burning forests and tornadoes. Climate change. It's not just in front of us—it's on top of us! But something is not adding up. Everyone I know is concerned about climate change, but somehow our politicians don't seem to be getting the message.

On the radio I listened to the commentary on a by-election win in Montreal by the ruling Liberal Party. Small wonder, it was held in the heavily anglophone, wealthy NDG-Westmount riding. Still, this is the same party that is building a new pipeline and approving new offshore oil exploration. The same party that has consistently failed to reduce our greenhouse gas emissions. Once again voters more concerned with language rights and ensuring that their MP is a member of cabinet have let the Liberals off the hook.

The other side of the aisle is no better, maybe worse. The Conservative Party's core support in the oil-producing provinces of Alberta and Saskatchewan has just gotten stronger since the election of its new firebrand leader. But all he and the prime minister do now is spar childishly in Parliament. When it comes to climate change, well, don't worry, the Conservatives' new boss tells us, the oil and gas industry is making wonderful technological advances in carbon capture. He reminds me of the spokespersons for the cigarette industry fifty years ago, trying to deflect the scientific research that had proven smoking causes cancer, but his poll numbers keep rising. As for the NDP, they are now so mired in identity politics that they have nowhere to go but down.

Is no one willing to take down the current regime of climate foot-draggers?

Of course, there are still the Greens, whom I've been helping since they dumped their crazy Quebec-bashing leader to bring back the old guard of committed environmentalists, but at four percent in the polls, they're not going to ignite a revolution anytime soon. Only the Quebec sovereigntists in the Bloc Québécois seem to have both the political discipline and the will to do something about climate change, but then they don't want to be part of a federal government. Not much help there.

The political scene is increasingly disappointing, and the environmental dangers are downright alarming. So, to alleviate my despair, I have lately taken up landscaping—an ambitious effort to turn my backyard into a French country garden, a place to drown my worries with a glass of pastis. I pride myself on sourcing things in an environmentally positive way: a lot of used pavers, free soil, rocks, plants and even trees from Facebook Marketplace. I have become quite the digital wheeler-dealer and master of re-purposing materials otherwise destined for the landfill. Plus, the garden has become a veritable carbon sink, or so I tell myself. Of course, I dodge the question of how much gas my 1997 Mercedes has used driving to the outskirts of Ottawa and Gatineau to get all these materials.

It's only a four-cylinder, but I feel a pang of guilt for postponing retiring it in favour of a new electric vehicle. Everyone has to do their part, I keep telling people, but my attachment to the old Merc keeps getting in the way of doing mine.

My new garden brings me lots of pleasure, a retreat from the outside world, but not everyone agrees. One friend tells me that I am not really being green by putting in all these pavers to create my raised garden beds, water fountains and patios. Instead, she says, I should let the weeds grow! She is very good at growing weeds. That I cannot do. My weeding fork is always at the ready to destroy the tiniest dandelion. I pluck each one with great relish, for I am a creature nurtured by a society that values a perfect lawn! Those weeds have become a real thorn of contention between us. But she is not fooling me. She is a fake Green. I know she has secretly been voting Liberal as part of a multi-generational tradition, ever since Pierre Trudeau welcomed her family to Canada. And as for those weeds, laziness is the apparent answer. Bad habits, like dandelions, die hard, but I am still intent on converting her to the cause.

Speaking of the Greens, I am now a party member. I was more or less guilted into joining the party to justify my criticism of the last party leader, who seemed hell-bent on single-handedly destroying the party during her short-lived reign. It is a small party in which many people cannot separate activism from practical politics. There are still animal rights activists who would expel other members for eating a hamburger, others who would bring down the party over a misused pronoun and some who see Canada as an oppressive colonial white patriarchy that must first be destroyed before we can reduce greenhouse gas emissions. At the same time, they all want a well-funded federal government that can afford guaranteed income payments to every citizen. The mass media, especially the CBC, love the dichotomies within the party. We are a cornucopia of misstatements and gaffes that make for good headlines on slow news days. And yet there is something endearing about being Green, or at least Green-ish.

Recently I spoke with Elizabeth May, the iconic leader of the party, at a Green event in Montreal. I am now sixty-eight, one year younger than her, making us contemporaries. She was telling me how her husband's ranch in Ashcroft, B.C., was almost burned down by wildfires last year, and how his daughter, who had gone there to activate the fire sprinkler system, ended up in the hospital with smoke inhalation. She also tried to tell me that Ashcroft was the only desert in B.C., but being born and raised in the province, I corrected her, saying that Osoyoos in the Okanagan also has a desert. Greens are true sceptics, so Elizabeth was quick to Google it on her phone. A typical reaction: Greens are good at agreeing on how horrific things are for the climate, and yet they are also terrible at trusting each other. But it was all good. We had a great chat, and anyway, the way things are going, it won't be long before all of Canada could be a desert.

My phone screams. I glance at it quickly. A new tornado warning, this time headed right for me. Shit! I wonder if this is how it's going to end: sitting in my basement as my house collapses on top of me, the pavers in my yard swept up into the vortex only to be launched like missiles into the neighbouring houses. The sky begins to darken, hail falls, and I shudder at the thought of my Mercedes being scarred by the icy pellets. I really need to clean out my garage to house it on days like this.

Then, like clockwork, the power goes out. I sit in the darkness of my recently renovated house, admiring my new orange leather couch. Leather, yes, another reason to get cancelled by the Green Party. And orange not green? Oh, well, maybe I am a subversive after all. The hail has now turned to heavy rain, so heavy that I can't see anything outside. Is this what an atmospheric river looks like? I pray for the good fortune of living on a hill, far enough away from the river to know that my house is impervious to flooding. Or so I tell myself. I fend off eschatological musings and look for a silver lining. Yes, my yard will be greener when all this is over, and maybe a few more people will call for action on climate change. We live in hope until we don't.

ENDANGERED SPECIES

Caroline Vu

I remember Switzerland. I remember the lakeside village of Gland. I remember its trees overhanging neat lawns. Beeches. Spruces. Pines. Maples. I counted them all. I remember the view from my cubicle. No, not Lake Geneva. No snow-capped Alps. Only an old sign flapping in the wind: Reserved Parking for IUCN Employees. I remember my colleagues. Three new eager faces. The others at home. Zooming in, zooming out. I preferred biking to the office. Our Red List kept us busy that month. Too many endangered species. More and more every year. Enumerating their fates troubled me. I lost sleep. We assessed 76,199 species. Of those, 42,108 species were endangered and 24,120 threatened with extinction. Analyze the numbers. Give the statistics a narrative. We did our job. "African elephants endangered due to poaching for ivory . . . Andean bears population decreasing because of inappropriate land use by the drug trade . . . Asian cheetah population down by eighteen percent since the rise in tourism . . . ." Yes, we gave each animal a face, a story.

CLL. Chronic Lymphocytic Leukemia. Stage Four. White blood count: 400,000. Median survival rate: one-point-five years. The statistics are worrisome. Family history: Nil. Exposure to insecticides: Not known. Cigarettes: None. Alcohol: None. Profession: Math teacher. My twin sister. Forty-seven years old. Weight lost: twenty-two kilos. Weight now: thirty-seven kilos. The numbers dishearten me. It is too much to grasp, yet not enough. Not enough to tell a story.

I remember IUCN. Our International Union for Conservation of Nature. I remember scientists reporting from all over the world. I remember long hours spent studying their research. I remember endless discussions on biodiversity loss. The urgency, the need to act fuelled our spirits. We wrote late into the night, drew graphs, dumbed down the science. Our Red List spoke for all the dying animals. We truly believed in it. We felt responsible for ensuring their survival. We took pride in protecting their habitats.

I'd left her four years ago. She didn't understand my obsession with endangered animals, my concern for the environment. "Switzerland! That's just an excuse to run away from our widowed mother! Your family should come before a bunch of monkeys! Flying here, flying there. What's so green about that?? You wouldn't be so eager to go if this IU-whatever was headquartered in a Third World country!" We never spoke again after that night. I sent her a postcard from Geneva. Another from Gland. An invitation to visit me. To hike the Swiss Alps together. She never answered. Never told me of her health problems. We were so close once.

My sister smiles seeing me. She tries talking. But her parched lips can't part. Her frozen tongue can't wag. Still smiling, she closes her sunken eyes. Her breathing stays calm. Her morphine-soaked body shows no traces of pain. The Montreal cold no longer bothers her. Our mother is slumped on a hospital chair near the door. Mom looks older than her seventy-two years. Her sparse white hair hardly covers her head psoriasis. Black circles surround her eyes. She waves me over. Whispers in my ears, "Agent Orange." The words fly about like a ping-pong ball in my head. Numbness creeps up my limbs. "What did you say?" I ask. Mom avoids my eyes, turns her gaze to the curtain-less window. She points to the snowflakes billowing outside. This gesture reassures me. Perhaps I'd misheard her words. "You want orange juice?" I ask. "No," she mumbles. She coughs, then chokes on her tears. "Agent Orange. The '70s. Vietnam. War. Dangerous chemicals. Poisoned lakes. Was pregnant with you two. Yes, pregnant with you two. She's last to come out. So small. Half your weight. A sickly child for many years. Now she's dying in our places. Dying for us." I stammer hearing the revelation, "Which lake? When exactly? Why didn't you tell me before? Why the secret all these years? Did she know? Anyone else affected in the village?" So many questions. No answer. Only cloudy eyes meet mine. "Dying for us" rings in my ears. Dying for us. Dying for us. Dying for us. I can't lower its volume. I caress my sister's emaciated face. My knees shake. Dizzy, I fall on the floor.

I remember Switzerland. I remember Gland. I remember my small studio. Posters of endangered turtles on a wall. Fern plants on the windowsill. A single bed in a corner. A tight space to share hugs. Like we did in our mother's womb. But she never came. My Agent Orange sister dying in my place. Carrying the burden for me. The burden of history. The weight of a deadly chemical. There must be others like her. Many others. I can imagine them—a generation of Agent Orange Sisters and Brothers. An endangered species no one talks about. No Red List to warn the world of their disappearance. No statistics to tug at our conscience. How can I tell their stories?

WILD GEESE

Sang Kim

Father looked innocent enough in those days, and never more so than when we were fishing in the gorge. He'd lean back in his folding chair on one side of the Hole, marking his floater on the river's surface, and recall happier times in the old country when he and the other men chased *gulbi* down the Han. They'd return days later in trawlers teeming with enough catch to feed the village many times over. These were the days before runoffs from city sewers leached into the ancient wells, before Sister and I came along, and when Mother must have still been in love with him.

Within too short a time, Mother didn't much mind Father's fishing escapades. She'd visit her friends at the Osan Air Base, where she once worked as a hostess at the Stars & Stripes Saloon during the unrest and where she also met Father, who was an interpreter for American fighter pilots. Sometimes she'd stay for a few nights, but always made sure to return home before the trawlers did. Villagers clucked on about her slipping back into the village under cover of darkness, her red stilettos hooked in hand and tugging at the hem of her miniskirt with the other. Father never paid much attention to any of it. A gossiper, he'd often tell Sister during our high school years, was like *budae chigae*, simmering with Spam, blood sausage and other nasty bits that smelled better than it tasted and was liable to cause indigestion.

While fishing, Father could forget about his job as a fryer at KFC —where he picked up a trick or two on ways to keep chicken meat moist—and ease into a childlike reverie. And though he wasn't one for many words, he sometimes said things to us then that have stayed with me to this day. After baiting Sister's hook or cutting my snagged line, he'd sit back on his haunches, and after a few drags of his cigarette, speak as though he'd been turning things over in his mind for some time. Sister accused him of reading too many books and referred to his random remarks as "gobbledygook." Father would smile, scratch his stubble with the nub of his missing index finger and respond with, "It's just common sense."

The summer before the incident I am about to describe, a family crossed over from the American side of the gorge. At a narrow pinch in the river, where a recent windstorm had brought down a giant spruce, a passable bridge had formed. We had already cast our lines when we saw them cutting a route through a knot of honeysuckle. Father rose, and, with his hands pressed against his thighs, bowed deeply to the old man in the group as though he were a figure of some distinction. The old man's fringed buckskin jacket brought to mind those people in the news who were always causing trouble for the oil companies and who Mother called a bunch of good-for-nothing drunks, but who Father believed were just folk defending what rightfully belonged to them. The old man returned Father's bow with a wave and turned to say something to the old woman, who nodded gravely. The three girls returned Father's bow in unison, giggling among themselves. The old man walked over to one of the fallen trees, dug through the tangle of branches and pulled out what appeared to be an almost intact bird's nest. It was at least three feet across and made of twigs, plant stalks and pieces of bark. He then peered up at some of the standing white pine, before heading our way.

"Used to be you saw a lot of birds around here," he said. "And salmon, too."

"Where are the salmon now?" Father said.

"They don't run anymore because of the dams." He pointed north, around the bend in the river. "But there are still a few spawning grounds left just up a-ways." Sister and Mother were at the picnic table watching the old woman and the girls on their knees washing their faces and necks in the river. The way Sister leaned her head in toward Mother, you could tell she was making a joke about it. When the family moved on, Father called Sister over to the Hole. A throbbing vein crawled up behind his right ear like a fat worm. I could tell something she did was bothering him. She stood over him with her arms crossed and her right foot tapping the ground while he rigged a new line and closed a lead shot with his teeth. Then he lit a cigarette, looked in the direction the family had gone and took a long drag. He said, "We live along the border of honesty and kindness. We just need to choose which side we're on."

"There he goes again with that gobbledygook," Sister said. She spun around and returned to join Mother at the picnic table.

When Father was laid off from KFC because of the lockdown, a rift began to form in our family. Without understanding much of it then, I found myself on one side of it with Father, and Sister on the other side with Mother. Each day the rift grew wider, so that by the end we'd arrived at a point where all but the most necessary words were exchanged between us.

Little things seemed to get under Mother's skin, like when Father's cigarette smoke drifted into the living room from the balcony or when he took up too much room on the kitchen floor to can left-over vegetables. But it was especially when the Lee family's name came up at the dinner table that a serrated edge entered Mother's voice. The Lees lived on the tenth floor, three below ours, and they received landed status the same year we did. But it didn't take long before they mysteriously amassed a fortune and moved away to a gated community in Richmond Hill, never to be heard from again. How they did this when they had no real business to speak of became the talk of our community. Rumours spread of a lottery win and how each of them made blood vows to never speak of it outside the family. But it was Mother who held a different view.

"It's about dreaming big dreams," Mother said to Sister across the table, "and hard work." Mother believed that the whole point of the refugee's life was to move from poverty to wealth as quickly as possible, by any means necessary. "You scoop up the golden eggs as quickly as they're laid."

During the pandemic, Father earned money by repairing appliances for the congregants of our church. Mother continued to work at the massage parlour, even though provincial health restrictions forbade such practices. "Massage is an essential service," she said. Sometimes, she'd come home early, change into a dress and run off with her Vietnamese boss, who was waiting downstairs in his Mercedes-Benz. Father pretended to be fixing something out on the balcony and never spoke about it.

When the lockdown was partially lifted, Sister packed her clothes into a duffle bag and went to stay with her boyfriend, who lived in his parents' basement out in the east end. I was happy to have our bedroom to myself, and even happier to resume my Air Cadets training classes twice a week. I had recently been promoted to the rank of Corporal in the 180 Mosquito Squadron and was working to earn a flying scholarship because I knew my parents couldn't afford to pay for it themselves.

Father once dreamed of becoming a fighter pilot but was deemed unfit because he was missing three fingers on his right hand from an IED he picked up during an anti-government protest. After training classes, I'd return home to find him alone reading a book or cutting out pictures from one of his many wildlife magazines and pasting them into a photo album. After dinner, I'd retreat to my bedroom to do my homework, and there, framed by the bedroom window, he'd be standing on the balcony smoking a cigarette. Later, when he was asleep on the sofa, I'd cover him with a blanket and tidy up around him. Once, I found an issue of *Field & Stream* open to a page about surviving in the woods with just a hunting knife. Father owned a fixed-blade Gerber that was gifted to him by the base commander at Osan. He always kept it strapped to his belt in a leather sheath whenever we went fishing. The handle, made from the antlers of an Indian stag, was the same smoke-stained colour of Father's teeth. The blade was seven inches long, with enough heft to do some damage if you were ever in a pinch.

When the lockdown was finally lifted, Mother and Sister were home more often than not, and for a brief time, there was a feeling of lightness in the apartment. I hoped that we'd see better days now that Father was back at work and the world was returning to some kind of normal again.

That fall, we took what I knew even then would be our last trip together to the gorge. It was an unseasonably hot October day, and the Pinto boiled over just outside the city. Smoke streamed out from under the hood, so Father pulled onto the shoulder. He and I walked to the nearest gas station, a mile or so away, to fetch some coolant. On the way back to the car, we stopped to watch rafts of geese fly overhead in shifting V-formations, honking as they went. They were coming down from the north where the lakes were starting to freeze over and where the cold drove them to seek warmer climates.

"They mate for life, you know," Father said, shading his eyes with his good hand. We walked on in silence, and I kicked a dented Coke can along the road's shoulder.

"You still remember our village?" he said after some time, then added, "You ever wish we could have stayed?" I told him I remembered some parts but not others and that it would have been too dangerous to stay while the General was still in power. I also thought there was no point in staying when Father had no family to speak of and Mother's side cut ties with her once she became pregnant with us. But I didn't say anything because I didn't want to put a damper on the day.

"Never mind," he said. "Memory is a narcotic." He put his arm around my shoulder and laughed. For the rest of the way to the gorge, Father drove slowly, with one eye on the temperature gauge. Through the rearview mirror, I could see Mother and Sister asleep, their heads holding each other up the way you saw seals doing it on a beach in those nature documentaries. I propped my elbow out the window and dreamt about the fish I'd catch. I imagined Father cutting out a photograph of me holding a monster muskie from *Field & Stream* magazine and proudly pasting it into his album.

The parking lot on top of the escarpment was empty except for a pickup truck near the boarded-up, hot-dog shack. We made our way cautiously down the steep, winding stairs. Mother and Sister led the way, both carrying IKEA bags full of blankets and sweaters. Each year, Mother carried less and less, complaining that the stairs were too much for her knees, even though she worked out at her boss's private gym almost every day and was as fit as any thirty-year-old. Father and I strapped folding chairs to our backs and held on to opposite ends of the icebox, heavy with food and drink. Down below, the wind stirred the tops of trees. Shoals of white waves crashed against boulders jutting out of the river. We used a scale from one to ten to measure the wind speed according to how choppy the water was.

"Five!" Father said across the icebox.

"Light breeze!" I replied, which was always the best condition for fishing. The sun was already high over the escarpment, with wisps of cirrus clouds smeared across it. The edges of Mother's chestnut curls shimmered in the light, and with her youthful figure, it was easy to imagine Father falling in love with her when they were young and didn't know any better.

Two men in camo hunting caps and matching wading pants stood knee-deep in the river near the landing. They were casting into an area where the water foamed around a cluster of cattails, and, from the type of jig spin they were using, I could tell it was for walleye or smallmouth bass, which were still around at this time of year. Father always released the walleyes, no matter how meaty they were because Mother didn't like the oily taste of them. When Father took off his Tilley hat and shouted hello, one of the men nodded his head and the other one touched the visor of his cap before turning away.

Mother and Sister laid a blanket on the grass beside a picnic table and went about setting up the barbecue. Father and I carried our chairs and fishing gear to the Hole, which was half a football field upriver.

The Hole was on this side of a high retaining wall that marked the bend in the river and was overgrown with green alder. It was curved like a horseshoe, about twenty feet across at the widest, with a narrow mouth that opened into an unhurried part of the river. Its banks sloped sharply up to a grassy knoll. Along the rim of the Hole, where it was shallow, water beetles and small fry scudded around floating leaves. But at its centre, where it was deep and still, the tail of some mysterious creature sloshed the surface then disappeared back into the depths. Father said it was likely an old cock that had finished spawning and come into the Hole to die.

We climbed up the bank and onto the knoll. Below us, a family of wood ducks waddled anxiously out of the bush and into the river. We tied up wing bobbers with imitation minnow plugs and cast out to an area where shark-fin rocks sliced through the water. The salmon liked to hang out there. We let the lure drift and watched the float bouncing off the rough waves every few feet. When it reached the next riffle downriver, we reeled in and cast again. We did this for about half an hour but weren't getting any action, so Father suggested we take a break. He rolled a cigarette and blew smoke into the wind. It occurred to me then that I hadn't seen him smile in a long time and hoped it might last until the next day and all the days to come.

By the time I became aware of it, the cabin cruiser had already made its way halfway up the river, creating huge swells in its wake. It was a *Sea Force*, about thirty feet long, a double-decker, the type you saw on the cover of those glossy magazines Mother brought home from work. It looked out of place on the river and made everything around it look shabbier than it actually was. Mother and Sister stopped what they were doing and stood at the river's edge gawking at it.

The cruiser stopped and anchored in the middle of the river, directly across from the picnic area. There were six people on board, two of them boys about my age. Father climbed on top of a boulder in his flip-flops and waved his hat at them, but either nobody on the boat saw him or they just chose to ignore him. Long strands of hair kept whipping into his face, and the light from the sky coloured the bald part of his head the same coral as spawning sockeye.

The boys were at the boat's prow strapping fighting harnesses on around their waists, two deep-sea fishing rods by their sides. Two women and two men were in a large open area towards the stern, the women lying back in lounge chairs. There was laughter coming from that end of the boat, followed by a squeal from one of the women, followed by more laughter. Reggae music was playing loudly in the background, the kind Sister turned on in our room when she was chatting with her boyfriend on the phone.

I watched as one of the boys hooked something, and from the way his rod bent it looked to be a ten-pounder, probably a Coho. They were jumping around the deck, hollering in the direction of the adults. One of the men appeared, a cigar jammed into his mouth.

"Drive her, Ray!" the man shouted. "Don't let her get away!" the other boy said. The rod jerked back and forth, and, from the look on Ray's face, he seemed surprised by the violence of it all. The man took the rod from the boy and worked his way uneasily toward the front of the boat, holding the railing with his free hand.

"Jack, haul your ass over here," he yelled over his shoulder. "It's a mother." The other man appeared, holding a can of beer in his hand. He put the beer down, picked up the net and went down on his knees above the ladder. The man with the cigar kept yanking the rod hard over his right shoulder, and the two boys stood around cheering him on. It ended as quickly as it started, and when Ray hauled it in with the net, I couldn't tell how heavy it was but knew I was right about it being a Coho.

The women were now also standing around watching. One of them daintily patted the man's face with a towel and said something to him while the other one laughed. The fish must have been flopping around on the deck because I could see the two boys kicking and stomping on it. Finally, the boys held it up from both ends and posed for photographs. Father watched it all, standing there on the edge of the knoll. The bottom of his cargo shorts flapped around his pale skinny legs like a flag whipping around a flagpole. He cupped his hands over his mouth and yelled, "Great job!" which the wind snapped up and carried away, so nobody could hear him.

Father turned to me and said he had an idea, then cut both our lines with his Gerber knife. He opened the tackle box and switched the minnow plugs for rainbow-coloured spinner baits with brush tails and trailer hooks. I knew this meant it was open season for all kinds of fish, not only the salmon, and that got me excited. I had a feeling now that something big was going to come our way. I pulled back the drag lever, held the rod over my shoulder and whipped my arm forward. It went out about thirty feet, and I let the lure run close to the surface, twitching the rod every so often to get a good spin on the willow leaf blade. Almost immediately I got a few strikes and managed to pull in two small steelheads—a three-pounder and five-pounder—without breaking a sweat. I slipped the smaller one back into the river and tossed the larger one on the grass in case nothing bigger came our way. Father was having no luck, but he kept on encouraging me.

When the smoke from the pig feet Mother was grilling drifted our way, I felt suddenly hungry. It was one of my favourite dishes and one of the few Mother knew how to make well. An ex-boyfriend of hers, a GI from Tennessee, had taught her the recipe during her days at Stars & Stripes. Father pulled out his Gerber again, cut out a Y-shaped stick from a tree branch, and speared it into the grass. I cast one more time and rested my rod where the two arms of the stick merged. Father reeled his line in because he didn't want to return to find it snagged under a rock or tangled in one of the tree roots along the bunker. I held the five-pounder by its gills and carried it back to the picnic area with me.

The cabin cruiser was now anchored on our side of the river. Sister was already on the deck chatting with the women, and Mother was being helped up the ladder by the cigar man, who was holding on to her hand and elbow.

"Whatcha catch?" It was Ray, the one who had hooked the fish.

"Just a steelhead," I said, holding it up.

"Hey, how'd you land a big one like that?" he said. He turned around to face the other boy, and I could tell he had a smirk on his face. "Weren't we using something like that for bait in Florida, Lou?"

"Even bigger," Lou said. "That's just barracuda bait, far as I'm concerned."

Father put his hand on my shoulder.

"My son is a great fisherman," he said. He pointed at Lou with the nub of his finger. "Just like you."

The man with the cigar appeared beside the boys and stared for a long time at Father's hand. "Don't be knocking it, Lou," he said, "It takes a lot of skill to catch them fast little critters."

"Must be some ancient Chinese secret," Lou said. The two boys looked at each other and smiled.

"We're not Chinese," Father said, raising his voice over the music. "We are Korean." I felt my face getting hot. A new song burst out from the back of the boat, and the cigar man yelled over his shoulder, "Turn it up, Jack!" The women began to grind their bodies up against each other. Sister stood to one side, swaying to the music.

"Anyways, we're all one, right?" the cigar man shouted at us. "One love, mahn!" he said, raising his beer.

"Yes!" Father said. "All one!"

"Better watch your barbecue over there. That meat'll turn into tires." Father and I turned around to see the grill engulfed in flames. I dropped the steelhead on the ground and we both ran over to the grill. Father pulled on the handle with his good hand, then immediately drew it back and wiped it on his shorts. For a moment, he stood over the grill clapping his hands together like a pair of mismatched cymbals, but the flames only grew bigger. I went over to the ice box, emptied it of the beer and dragged it over toward the grill. Together, we lifted it and poured the ice and water over the flames. A plume of white smoke poofed all around us. I jumped away, coughing. Father covered his mouth with the crook of one elbow and pulled one of the pig's feet off the grill. It was so charred you couldn't tell which part was hoof and which part meat.

It was at that moment my rod fell off the Y stick and the knoll and was being dragged along the shoreline, toward the retaining wall. If the rod got past the wall, I knew it would be lost for good. I raced towards it and grabbed the handle just as it was being pulled into the river. The spool was still shrilling and had almost run out of line, so I locked down the reel. The rod bent hard, the tip jiggling erratically. This was a monster, easily a twenty-pounder, much bigger than anything I'd caught before. I waded slowly back out of the water and held the rod out for Father, who was waiting on the shoreline, out of breath. The fish was around the bend, on the other side of the retaining wall, so we couldn't see anything except the taut line. Father alternately pulled and released the rod and reeled furiously. But there was something unusual about the way the line zigzagged through the air. It was jerking haphazardly, suddenly down, then sideways, as if the fish had failed to scale a waterfall and kept tumbling back into the river or bouncing off rocks. This was followed by a violent thrashing sound, which was different from the sound salmon usually make when they catch air and fall back into the water. It continued to fight hard, but Father had the rod firmly in both hands. He walked slowly into the water, like the way you saw those pros do on television. But when the water reached up to his waist, he pushed his way back to the shoreline. His legs were pink from the cold water. The rod was now bent completely out of shape, so he gave out some line and let the fish run. For a moment, he appeared stumped, out of ideas, but then pushed his way around some hemlock and over a stump of a tree. He climbed up an embankment on this side of the retaining wall, but one of his flip-flops slipped off and drifted downriver, and the wind swept his hat off his head. Everybody was crowded together on one side of the boat to watch. Even the men in the camo waders stopped what they were doing to follow the action. The gorge fell silent.

Father finally managed to make his way to the top of the embankment. He held on to a branch of a tree with his left hand, and with his other arm extended, held the rod as far as he could toward the river's bend. But the line got tangled somewhere. He yanked the rod as hard as he could and suddenly the line snapped. The rod slashed backward through the air, and the momentum thrust Father down the slope toward the Hole. He ended up near the mouth of the Hole. Then I heard a strange noise coming from the other side of the retaining wall. More of the thrashing noises. I stood frozen in place and waited, my heart thumping through my wet shirt. The white fishing line, coiled together in some parts, drifted on the river's surface. This was followed by a dark lump. At first, I couldn't make out what it was because dusk had already begun to set in the gorge. When it finally came into view, the object turned on its side and pirouetted in weak circles, occasionally thwacking a wing against the water. Father rose slowly from where he was. I could hear him breathing through his nose. And to this day, I'll never forget the expression on his face. It was like a night shot on the African savannah—of a gazelle caught in the camera's flash. The look of hunted prey.

The goose was struggling to stay afloat, its head jerking in and out of the water. Father dove into the water after it. He dog-paddled from rock to rock, white water slashing at him from all sides. At some moments, he'd completely disappear, only to resurface five or ten feet downriver. Where it was still and the current formed small whirlpools, the goose turned in circles. Father reached out with his good hand and snatched the goose by its tail. The goose arched its long black neck, snapped once at Father's arm, before it drooped languorously to its side. After what felt like hours, Father managed to get to a shallow rocky area about fifty yards away from me, hauling the goose behind him. I went into the water after him and held on to his free arm. He laid the goose gently on the grass, and I saw that its eyes were gleaming like soaked black beans.

Suddenly, with one final gasp, the goose attempted to stand, its neck cartoonishly undulating. It beat its wings wildly before collapsing to the ground. Bits of down drifted in the air. With its black neck fully exposed, I could see tiny droplets of blood gurgling out from a spot under its beak and the silver leader dangling out of its mouth. Father held the beak open with his thumb and forefinger and tried to pry the spinnerbait out. But it was in too deep. He sat back on his haunches with his head drooped forward between his bony shoulders. From the way his body was convulsing, it looked like he may have caught a chill from being in the water too long. When he finally rose, the dead goose was cradled in his arms. He turned in the direction of the dark woods. In his good hand, glinting by his side, was the Gerber knife.

An olive moon crimped along the river's surface. Downriver, the red stern lights from the cabin cruiser disappeared behind a mist descending into the gorge. The stench of dead fish hung thick in the air. Each time a bat banked sharply over her head, Sister clasped her arms around mother and whimpered like a bullied child. Mother just sat there, impassive and ramrod straight, staring past me. Flames from the barbecue grill flickered on the lenses of her sunglasses.

At last, Father placed the aluminum foil pan in the centre of the picnic table and quietly took his seat beside me. Expertly cut slices of the goose's breast were layered one on top of the other, its pearly flesh gleaming against the charred skin. He transferred portions onto paper plates and set it before each of us. I ate right away even though I wasn't feeling hungry, even though the blood stench of something that had just died made me feel nauseous. I knew even then that shovelling food down my throat was merely a temporary salve to fill a growing cavity inside me, one that I would come to terms with only after everything in our lives came apart.

"I'm going to be sick," Sister said, rising from the table. She staggered toward the woods with one hand covering her mouth and threw up over a dogwood bush. The sound of her retching was nullified by the cacophony of chirring crickets. Mother didn't eat. She sat there, still as a statue. From the corner of my eye, I caught a glimpse of her face, gaunt and no longer putting up the usual fight against her age. She took on the appearance of those Apache women warriors in sepia photos, staring into oblivion. And reflected off the convex curve of her sunglasses was Father's distorted head—the wide forehead, the pencil-thin sharp chin and those too-wide searching eyes. They looked like the eyes of wild geese about to take flight, about to embark on a long journey to some unknown destination.

THE ANARCHIST

Jerry Levy

I took a flying leap and struck the bank's pane of glass with the heel of my Doc Martens. It fanned out in a splintered mosaic but didn't break. I removed a crowbar from my backpack and whacked. Once, twice . . . the third time, shards of glass fell to the ground. Buoyed by cheers and gasps from onlookers, I reared back one final time and watched as more glass accumulated at my boots. Then I slipped back into the anonymity of the large crowd.

I had to find my comrades. They were easy to spot: dressed in black with balaclavas, we agreed to meet at the horse statue in Queen's Park just after eight p.m.

Comrades. It's a trendy moniker, I realize. We're just kids though, mostly in our teens and twenties. Students, artists, writers. Many are unemployed or scraping by with odd jobs. A few bike couriers. What we have in common is anger. There's not a single one of us that isn't pissed off at something. Mostly about the state of the environment. What sort of world our kids will inherit. So we set fires, overturn cars, kick in glass. Demonstrations are where we work best. Like G20 summits. We run amok and, when the time is right, discard our black clothing in a heap.

There we sat, a baker's dozen, passing around joints and drinking beer. Listening to reggae music from someone's iPhone. I suppose some people might say that thirteen is an unlucky number, but I don't see it that way—these people are all the family I really have.

My mother is not well, and I take care of her. Alzheimer's. It's a terrible disease. Many days she doesn't even recognize me. And my old man, well, he's been out of my life a long time. I've really been on my own for years. So, if I'm petulant and angry, then, well, can you blame me? But here, among others who have similar stories to tell, I fit right in. I just want to stand arm in arm with them and rebel. Burn society for not putting my name on the guest list for the G20.

My name is Shandy. Most everyone calls me Shan. I was born twenty-six years ago to a petroleum engineer and a jazz singer. For all I know, my father may still be an oil and gas guy, connecting pipelines or installing some thingamajig in refineries. Always the environmentalist. Ha! Why should he care about the state of the environment when the money rolls in?

Shandy, right? It's not your typical name but my parents gave it to me, go blame them. Really, blame the old man. My mother wanted to name me Sade, after the singer, and him, well, he was always stuck on Andy—even for a girl—after his own name. They couldn't agree on much, this being one of those times, and so "Shandy" was a dumb compromise.

We lived in Mississauga, just west of Toronto. It's a little like Mayberry, that fictional TV town, inhabited by homespun folks who spend tranquil evenings rocking on front porches and who are about as interesting as quadrangles in geometry class. Yes, another superlative amalgamation, triangle and quadrilateral. Go figure. I only know the show because when my mom started getting sick, she would watch it *ad nauseam*, saying in a quivering voice that it brought her a bit of levity, and some peace. Barney Fife, Andy, Aunt Bee, Opie, Goober. I can see them all now.

It was a middle-class existence, at least on the face of it. Inside was a different story. My father had old-world ideas about a woman's place in society. But my mom loved to sing (and dance) and wanted a different life. The night life. She adored Billie Holiday, Sade, Ella Fitzgerald and the Queen of Soul, Aretha. Bluesy, jazzy stuff, with just a touch of soul and gospel. She sang in church choirs, which my dad approved of. But when she expressed a desire to sing in nightclubs, an acrimonious battle set in. She'd sometimes get gigs at small clubs on Queen Street, opening for more well-known acts. On those occasions, he would read her the riot act and threaten to leave. He didn't frighten her, but since she had no money of her own, it was a threat she paid attention to.

Ah yes, money. We never wanted for it and had all we needed—the oil and gas business pays its employees well for screwing up the environment. There were nice clothes, a picturesque house (with a white picket fence, of course), cars, vacations in Europe and at five-star resorts in the Caribbean, fine restaurants, expensive furniture from the Art Shoppe on Yonge Street. But I grew up knowing it meant nothing, especially when I saw Mom crying, which was often. Then, when my father left on one of his business trips and never came back, it really hit home. He eventually did return, a new woman in tow, and hired the best divorce lawyer he could find. A parting of the ways was best, mom realized that, but like I said, she was scared. And with good reason. The bastard exaggerated, distorted and hid assets offshore. Without access to the kind of legal representation facing her, Mom ended up with little.

Still, it wasn't all bad. We moved into a small apartment on Eglinton Avenue, just above a Jamaican patty shop. It was clean, though a bit noisy from the whir of passing cars. Usually we kept the windows closed. I went to school, and she waitressed and pursued her lifelong ambition to sing. And sing she did, everywhere and anywhere she could. Sometimes I'd accompany her to shows, and I couldn't have been more proud. She was so damn good. We were a sisterhood, the two of us. But then the illness set in. Now I understood why she cried so often, and it had nothing to do with my father.

So, she's now at *that place*, that's what I call it, where they've put her for all time. Where sharp objects and matches are strictly forbidden, and patients are placated with small white pills and lemonade. It is where I lie in bed next to her, my arm around her tiny waist, my breathing shallow so as not to upset her with sounds from unwelcome visitors. These sounds, voices so unlike her own sultry one, which had the unique *vibrato timbre*. Hysterical pitches, that's what they are, screaming in her ear that she should be ashamed and that they are coming.

And they do come. She greets them with a solitary word: No! And I kiss her cheek and hold her hand, wipe the spittle from her mouth. There is nothing else. My lady has grown thin and gaunt in that place, plagued by voices from the apocalypse. Although her eyes are wide open, she can no longer see me.

That place. Where I loathe going. Where I have learnt that nothing is fair.

I took one last hit from a bong and stood up unsteadily. "Gotta go," I said, wiping a strand of wet hair from my forehead. "That was a real rush."

Gavin, our leader, grabbed my shoulders and kissed both cheeks. "Shan, I swear to God, ya did good. The sacred cows will take stock of the damage tomorrow and won't know what hit 'em." He held out a closed fist, which I touched with my own. "Ya want some smoke for the road?"

"Nah, I'm good."

And I was. I hadn't eaten since breakfast, and the weed had made me ravenous. Close to my house, I dumpster-dove into a bin behind a restaurant and came up with half a chicken, a loaf of rye bread, some wilting lettuce and a tin of mackerels. My lucky night. I sat down at a curb and made a sandwich.

I was in a state of numbness, a curious mix of subsiding adrenaline and apathy. It was the way I always felt after a day of lunacy. I chewed my sandwich absent-mindedly but perked up when I realized I was going home. Home! I'd be a hermit and paint for the next few days. Actually, Gavin says artists don't have to work for a living, that they're special people. If only I could sell a few of my paintings. Maybe I'd just read.

I do read a lot. Mostly books my comrades give me. It's for my "education." That's what they say. I know, for instance, that Churchill had it all wrong when he said capitalism is the worst system . . . except for all the others. Some of the others are indeed better. Like Marxism. Everyone knows the bourgeoisie exploits the working class. So the working class has to seize power through revolution and place production into some collective, then spread the wealth evenly. Rats like my deadbeat father have to be made examples of. Some say my friends and I are anarchists because we create havoc, but we're just bringing the capitalists to their knees. It's the first step toward a better world, where the environment comes first. Clean water, clean air.

Once my life was different. I excelled at school. I wanted Mom to be proud. I graduated with a degree in Economics from the University of Toronto and was hired into the management training program at a major bank. I was fast-tracked and on my way. But then I lost it all when I was charged with stealing change from the till. Why I did it, I can't say. Mom was getting progressively worse, and the stress was becoming intolerable. I started smoking, eating junk food. It's not an excuse for what happened, I know. But I was nearly out of my mind with worry and clearly not thinking.

I stole the princely sum of $126.25 over a period of a few months. I acknowledged my guilt, offered to pay the money back. Even resign. It was paltry and an internal matter, that's how I looked upon it. Disciplinary action was called for, and I was ready for it. But the bank called the police, which led to charges: "Theft of two hundred and under." I was placed on probation for six months. Ash and smoke darkened my star and made me unemployable in the world I had known, a virtual pariah. It was then I was reborn.

Artists, bike couriers, musicians, punks, anyone who doesn't abide by society's rules. Those are my people. In fact, after the bank, I got a job as a courier, delivering X-rays, engineering reports, legal documents and anything else that fits into my tattered shoulder bag.

The job takes me into the bowels of downtown Toronto, where I ride the wrong way on streets, through red lights, up on sidewalks, and down stairs, scattering pedestrians. If I'm feeling it, I hurl a basket of insults at car owners: "Think about the environment! Looks like you want to get your mirror broken driving in my lane!" Hey, but it's not only motorists who get it. Whenever I see someone on a cell: "Brain cancer, buddy." To a pack of vagrants hovering above a grate: "Millionaire's row, boys." To overweight people: "Gym time." Anyone in my way, and many who aren't.

I stand in elevators next to the suits, the very ones I used to hang with. Corporate drones, that's what I now think. Completely lacking in imagination, stupidly proud of the drab grey and blue suits they wear likes badges of honour! So there I am, adorned with nose and lip rings, tattoos running up my arms onto my neck, sweaty and smelly. Then, as I get off at a floor, I sometimes stick out my studded tongue, just for fun. Yeah, so I'm anti-corporate and anti-establishment. What about it? I'm an artist, after all. If I kick in a window, give someone the finger, scare a bunch of pedestrians, these are just splashes of bold colours that I add to the tapestry of my life.

I took a shortcut through a forested area. It was pitch-black but I knew the path. A flashlight helped light the way. The crickets were out in full throttle. To save time, I veered off the main path and walked through waist-high grass. I saw it then, a big green checkmark on a tree, an old growth tree that I had named Rumi after the poet, one that must have been hundreds of years old. Then other checkmarks on more trees. I knew what that meant. Not knowing what else to do and feeling especially tired from the insanity I wreaked during the day, when I got home, I took a couple of slugs of Jack Daniels and went to bed.

In the morning I woke sticking to the sheets, damp with night sweat. Had it all been some strange nightmare? That they were going to cut down Rumi and the other trees? But why?

I hung out with my fellow couriers at the Jet Fuel Café on Parliament Street and told them about Rumi. My revelation was met with groans.

"The City is building an LRT, and all the checkmarked trees are directly in their path," said a woman named Natasha.

Others chimed in with their thoughts, extolling the virtues of trees. Like how they eat greenhouse gases, clean the air, give a home to wildlife, provide people with oxygen, prevent landslides. My colleagues rattled off an almost endless list.

"But I've often sat under Rumi," I said. "She's covered in moss, almost like she's giving me a soft landing. I have to do something to save her. She trusts me."

"Ask Gav what he thinks," added Natasha.

I rode my bike like a fiend to Gavin's place, a first-floor bachelor apartment on Pape Avenue. I always thought the Confederate flag he used as a window covering was dumb, but at least it provided some colour—dark blue, red and white—to his otherwise drab olive green and brown living room furniture. It was always easy with him, as long as topics were on point: politics or the environment. He had a general disdain for everybody and anything not connected with his ideologies.

"Gav, it's awful," I said. "They're going to cut down all these beautiful trees. What do you think we can do?"

Gavin ran his hand over his bristly purple, blue and black Mohawk. It really was a work of art, I had to admit. "You know, Earth Day just passed," he said, "and since that first Earth Day in 1970, we've lost more than one billion acres of forest. What do you think of that, huh?"

I shrugged. "It's bad, Gav. Real bad. They're going to cut down these beautiful trees. Just for a stupid LRT. What should we do?"

"There's nothing for us to do except use violence. Violence draws attention to issues, trust me."

Outside, I banged my fist against the leather seat of my bike. A flat. Great. The sky had turned overcast and was spitting rain. I jogged with my crippled steed to a nearby bike shop where Sue

Taylor worked, a comrade-in-arms. I always liked Sue. Olive skin, full lips, soft brown curls. She looked more like a movie starlet than someone bent on sheer mayhem. But it was something about her easy-going nature—her controlled chaotic ways—that attracted me. An oxymoron? I don't think so. Whenever things got too heated, when there was too much damage or the possibility of some bystander getting hurt, she'd walk away. Or if she thought our motives for action were plain dumb, she wouldn't participate. Case closed.

"I make my point," she once told me, "and after that, anything else is for vultures like Gavin." I'm not sure if the exalted one ever heard her speak those words, but I do know he was never very big on Sue. "I'm close to being done with smashing windows and setting fire to cars," she said. "I just want a peaceful life."

The tube and tire needed to be changed. A double whammy. Using a pair of tweezers, Sue removed a shard of glass. "There you go, Shan, your kryptonite."

"How much is this going to set me back? I'm not exactly rolling in dough, as you know."

Sue smiled knowingly. "We'll figure something out."

I watched her work. She inserted a tire lever between the tire and the rim and quickly worked her way down. In seconds, the inner tube and rubber tire had been removed.

"No tread left, Shan," she said. "It was bound to happen."

While Sue fixed my bike, I drank coffee and munched on the homemade cookies she provided. "Even revolutionaries like chocolate chip cookies," she said.

I laughed. "Clever."

"Not mine, Shan. Straight out of 'Doonesbury'."

I began telling Sue how I felt after days of destruction—that I was numb, lonely and confused. Shivers of adrenaline morphed into anxiety. I hadn't planned on divulging all that. It just slid right out my mouth.

"I can't blame you."

"No?"

"Of course not. That's why I'm phasing out. Slowly, but I'm getting there."

"But I think the ideas Gav and others preach are good. They make perfect sense. A lot of times I'm hooked, and . . . ."

Sue stopped working and looked me straight in the eye. "Hey, hey, you're babbling." She took a rag and wiped her brow. "How old are you anyway?"

"Twenty-six."

"Well look, I'm thirty-five. I can't keep doing this forever. Going to the grave with my legacy being smashed windows, confrontations with cops, jail time and restitution. Uh, uh. Sam and I are trying to get pregnant."

"Sam Shillings?"

"Yes, that Sam. The guy with the blue bandana. Nice pecs, strong jawline."

We laughed.

"I had no idea you guys were an item."

"We try to keep it quiet. Like I do with this shop."

"What do you mean?"

"Shan, I'm one of the owners."

"Huh?"

"You're probably thinking Gav would kill me if he found out I turned into a capitalist pig."

"That's kind of what I was thinking."

"And that's why I don't say anything. Everyone knows I work here, they just don't know the details. Like who owns it. Anyway, let me tell you about our esteemed leader." Sue went on to reveal that

Gavin had a hard-core criminal background, having served time in a federal penitentiary for armed robbery. Pistol-whipped someone unnecessarily in the process. Furthermore, he had ties to motorcycle gangs.

"I never knew."

"He doesn't want you to know. He just wants you to hear about Marx and shit. He's a two-bit hood disguised as a radical for causes. All these environmental causes. But he doesn't really care. He uses all the environmental rhetoric to serve his own needs. A bad dude to his core."

"Interesting."

"Don't get me wrong. I think changes are needed in the system. Money is in the hands of too few. Lots of people get shafted. The environment gets shafted. It's just that, as I've gotten a bit older, my priorities have shifted. Violence doesn't always solve everything. I have come to the conclusion that diplomacy is a better route."

"Yeah, I think you're absolutely right. All this violence doesn't seem to have solved my life. And uh, just one more thing."

"Okay, what is it?"

"I want my Mom to be proud of me, the way she used to. She has Alzheimer's and isn't aware of what's going on. But still, maybe through all that haze, maybe she knows."

We walked to the front cash, and Sue put an arm around me. "You'll have to figure it out for yourself, kiddo. But if you ever need to talk . . . ."

"*Merci beaucoup*."

I paid the paltry twelve dollars I owed ("I'm the owner," said Sue, pulling on her coverall straps, "and I know my prices. Ha. Ha.") and walked out into the street. The rain had stopped, the sun was peeking through, and I rode back to my apartment.

A few days later, I was walking my bike through the forest on my way to my job as a bike courier. As I trod a path through the tall grass and saw that the trees had been felled. All the green-check-marked ones, including Rumi. I dropped to my knees and wept.

Gavin had called earlier. Another protest. This one along Bay Street, the heart of the financial district, ending up in St. James Park where some were planning to camp out in an effort to raise awareness about the devastating effects of environmental negligence. About corporate greed. The agenda, of course, included untold violence.

I hadn't planned on going, but I knew then and there that I had to go. For Rumi. I would be crazy, and God help anyone who tried to stop me.

GREEN TOE

Timothy Niedermann

It was spring, and I was mowing the grass for the first time that year. My lawn is too small for a sit-down mower and too large for a simple reel push model, so my machine is a self-propelled, twin-blade motorised number, perfect for keeping the grass at the right height. It's gas powered, because I can't deal with cords and charging. There's a limit. I also have a trimmer for keeping my bushes neatly groomed, with an edger attachment to sharpen up the borders of the flower beds.

My mind was going down the list of chores to get everything set for the year ahead, when I noticed a large clump of dandelions and made a mental note to get some weed killer at the hardware store. Then I felt a bump.

This was odd. I had always kept the lawn well-manicured, so it was extremely smooth. So what was this? It couldn't be a rock. A mole tunnel? That meant getting a trap. I looked down. My shoe was covered with blood. I pushed the mower away. It stopped automatically as I knelt down to examine the wound. My shoe was slashed open, and I could see that my big toe was only held onto my foot by a thick piece of skin.

That was when the pain began. As usual when I do yard chores, I had left my phone in the house to give me some peace. Squeezing my foot to stanch the blood flow, I yelled for my wife. "Karen! Help, I'm bleeding!" No answer. I waited and yelled again. "Karen!" Still no answer. The pain was growing, and it was hard to think straight. Not knowing what else to do, I began to crawl toward the house, one hand around my injured foot, the other on the ground for balance.

Leaving a smear of red behind me on the grass, I finally made it to the back stoop but couldn't climb the three steps leading up to the house. "Karen!" I called again. My head was starting to feel light as Karen finally opened the door and gasped "Jesus!" when she saw me. She bent over and helped me to sit up on the lowest step then pulled out her phone. "I'm calling an ambulance." As she spoke to the 911 operator, she sat down next to me and helped put pressure on my foot.

The ambulance came promptly. The EMTs bandaged my foot and wrapped it in a cold compress, then hooked me up to an IV and loaded me into the ambulance. Shock sensations were washing over me, and the technician riding next to me kept asking me questions to keep me awake.

In the ER an orderly checked my vitals and assured me I would be in surgery soon, as an OR had just opened up. He asked me if I needed anything. I shook my head. Nodding, he moved away to other patients.

As I lay there, I felt annoyed with myself. What a stupid thing to do! This would set the whole schedule back. I went over my spring yard checklist in my mind. There was a lot still to do. How long would it take for me to get back on my feet? Literally. I smiled internally at that one. This was all too much. I closed my eyes.

This was the time of year you had to move fast in the yard. Fertilize the lawn. Mulch the flower beds. Get ahead of the weeds—nuke them before they had a chance to spread. Order the annuals. Prune the roses. You had to cut roses back severely every year or they would send their long, spiked branches everywhere. A gangly mess, that would be. A well-clipped rosebush was a thing of beauty, but it took work. And I had several. All different colours.

My yard and flower garden were not overly elaborate. To me, devoting constant time and effort was needlessly obsessive. But it did have to be a source of relaxation, so it had to please the eye. I chose flowers that matured at different rates so there was always something blooming. Viburnum, tulips, lilacs, roses, peonies, hosta. Not huge amounts of any, just a smooth stream of colour through the summer and into the fall.

Then there was the lawn itself. It had to be immaculate. That damned dandelion would pay for what it did to my foot! There was nothing like sitting after work, cocktail in hand, looking out over a perfect lawn. A sort of neutral backdrop that didn't clash with what was in bloom. And that meant none of the crabgrass that was left for the whole rest of the year after the dandelions bloomed in the spring—unless you gave it a hefty dose of weedkiller first thing.

After a while, two orderlies came up and wheeled me down the hall and through several doors to the OR, where an anaesthetic was syringed into my IV. Seconds later I was unconscious.

I awoke in the recovery room and lay there as the anaesthetic's haze slowly dissipated.

When I was fully awake, orderlies checked me over and then wheeled me to a semi-private room. Not long after, a woman came in and introduced herself as Dr. Fields, the surgeon who had operated on me. She pulled back the sheets and examined the stitched-up wound.

"Looks good. I was able to reattach your toe. It should be painful for about a week. I'll give you a prescription to help with that. The nurses will put your foot in a small cast to keep the toe immobile while the bone heals. Shouldn't take more than four to five weeks or so. You will be supplied with a walking boot, but I wouldn't put too much pressure on the foot for the first couple of weeks, just to let the healing get a good start. Please schedule an appointment with me in about a month's time."

With that, she was gone. Nurses came in and put a thin cast around my foot. All I could see were the tips of my toes. Karen arrived about an hour later and took me home.

I would have to work from home for a while, but that wouldn't be a problem. Thanks to the pandemic, I was well versed in Zoom. Quite a switch for me, though. During the pandemic I was one of the first to go back to the office. I felt we managers needed to set an example. I wore a suit and tie as well. Nothing casual. The pandemic's effect on office discipline had been unfortunate while so many people worked from home, and I felt I needed to project the required level of professionalism, set the standard for when people returned to their desks.

My strong conviction was that the only way to succeed in life is to run a tight ship, at work and at home. Otherwise, things go to hell. Discipline. That was my mantra. The security of order and routine.

Now I had to develop a new daily pattern for myself. My commute was reduced to walking after breakfast from the kitchen to my home office, where I remained until after five except for lunch and bathroom breaks. I wore a jacket and tie as a matter of habit, but also to preserve that necessary air of office professionalism, even though I was working from home. I felt this was especially important to convey during Zoom calls.

At five, I would change clothes—this took a while—and pour myself a drink, which I carried out to the patio, where I would sit and wait for Karen.

Karen came home from her job around 5:30, depending on traffic. Usually we made dinner together, but, until my foot healed, there was little I could do except sit and chop vegetables. We decided to eat dinner in the kitchen instead of the dining room, so I wouldn't have to walk as much. We would go back to the dining room when my foot started feeling better.

The first week went by easily. The meds did the job on the pain, and though the toe was still tender, I was able to concentrate on my work quite well, all things considered. After work, on the patio, I enjoyed the tulips and the daffodils and wasn't too worried about the lawn. I would get to it soon if my foot kept progressing as well as it was.

By the second week, the yard was showing signs of enthusiastic spring growth. The trees were leafing out, creating the summer's shade, and the grass was thick and vibrant—and getting shaggier with each day. But the daffodils and tulips were soothing. Just to see their coloured petals calmed me no end.

"Why don't you hire someone to cut the lawn?" Karen asked me one evening.

"Because they wouldn't do it fucking right!" was my brittle response. I immediately apologised to her for being so sharp, but, as I tried to explain, I needed precision and attention to detail in my yard, not somebody who just zipped in and zipped out, the way those outfits did business. "It's just that I've put a lot of work into this yard, and I don't want anyone screwing it up."

This was my home, my patch of earth. I owned it, and it was going to be properly tailored to suit my needs. And I wanted it to be beautiful so when I came home from work I could relax. And it was going to be the way I wanted it, free of the damn weeds. Green and pristine. No flaws. Perfect.

There were limits, though. I had thought about planting boxwoods as a sort of mini hedge to frame the flower beds, but the spectre of all that additional clipping put me off. The roses were enough. The idea was to get things done in the spring and then relax and enjoy my disciplined parade of colour for the months that followed, not add yet another level to the yard chores.

My foot healed quickly. By the end of the first week the pain had dulled to a minor ache, and by two weeks, the wound was only slightly tender. I began taking brief walks outside using the walking boot, gingerly testing my limits.

By then, things were definitely behind schedule. My perennials were holding their ground, but violets had sprung up to pepper the grass with their little white-and-purple buds, crowding in among the round, yellow manes of the dandelions. I couldn't remember seeing so many of either before.

My frustration began to grow. There was so much to do that wasn't being done: weedkiller to spray and fertiliser to be spread, weeds to pull out, annuals to be planted and watered. I had my list, but there was no point driving to the local nursery (even if I could drive) and getting anything if I couldn't plant it immediately. There was just too much preparation to do first. Watering plants in their plastic flats was an additional chore I didn't need.

I found myself gazing out my home office's window a lot to check what was happening in the yard. All this did, however, was to remind me of all that wasn't being done. These thoughts began to interfere more and more with my work, so, to avoid the distraction, I decided to keep the room's curtains closed during work hours.

But afterward, sitting on the patio, far from being the source of calm it had always been, the yard became torture. It was a disaster.

My creation. My controlled space. The small sanctuary I had created for myself was being overrun by the chaos of nature. The clump of dandelions was still there, and it was not alone. Dozens of others had sprouted up around it, and their round, yellow blooms turned toward the patio, little faces laughing at me, taunting me.

My ability to move around improved steadily, so one afternoon, I went into my garden shed and hauled out my lawnmower. Bracing myself, I pulled on the starting cord. Again and again. Harder and harder. Finally, the engine started, but on that last pull I lost my balance and fell over, twisting my leg and snagging my foot. The pain was instantaneous and sharp.

At the hospital, the verdict was delivered soberly: "You have re-broken your toe."

This time healing took longer, and the pain was worse, so I got stronger meds, but my discomfort persisted longer than the first time. Gradually I started to feel better and move around more, testing the foot carefully. But just as I thought I was turning the corner, I woke up one day with my whole foot red and swollen. The hospital diagnosed an infection. More meds. The swelling took a week to come down. I tried to focus on work, but the constant aching shortened my attention span, along with my temper. I grew angry and distracted. Wearing a jacket all the time got to be a nuisance, so I dispensed with it, using the excuse that the warm temperatures of summer were approaching. Not long afterward, I stopped bothering with a tie. That raised some eyes on Zoom calls.

As the days and weeks passed and the discomfort lingered, work became impossible. I felt crippled, both in body and spirit. I started taking half days and whole days off to collect myself, but it was no use. Finally, I asked for a leave of absence until I was fully healed. This was granted.

The question now was what to do to pass the time while I healed. It was pointless to spend time in my home office, and I can't stand daytime television, so I decided to catch up on my reading. I had Karen buy me a set of Louise Penny mysteries, and this I felt was perfect, intelligent but not demanding. I didn't want to feel cooped up inside, so I took my books out to the patio and made myself comfortable. Taking a deep breath before opening the first volume, I took stock of the yard. The grass had grown very long. The amount of work needed to get the yard back in shape was becoming overwhelming, and for the first time I was tempted to hire a gardener, but for some reason I held off.

Reading on the patio worked well. The days passed pleasantly, and I got to know Inspector Gamache quite well as I worked my way through the series. But after a while I found myself raising my eyes from the page more and more to gaze out over the yard. I was staring at nothing, for the most part, but I slowly began to notice little, unexpected things.

The daffodil petals had browned and fallen off, leaving their green stalks like thicker stands of grass and little bits of yellow were rising among them. I squinted and then remembered. Buttercups! I hadn't seen or even thought of buttercups since I was a kid. I didn't remember them as so tall, but there they were.

The yellow heads of the dandelions had turned into little fuzzy globes of white seed tufts, which were taken by the wind, soaring up over the lawn. Some fell as I watched, others soared out of view, riding the wind to conquer another lawns.

What was my yard now? A mess of thriving vegetation. Mostly grass, yes, but with other unfamiliar plants popping up unexpectedly. Strange bugs zipped around, and bird calls filled the air. It was a concert of abundance, and it began to give me joy.

As the grass reached full height and the seed heads formed, each stalk would sway with the wind. I found this rhythmic movement calming, and the pain slowly waned, as if the soft breeze were blunting its edge. My thoughts, usually centered on work, wandered places they hadn't been in a long time, aimlessly remembering people and places that life had squeezed from my conscious mind. I watched the bees flit from blossom to blossom, fulfilling their role as pollinators. Birds I had never seen before flew in and out of the trees, many chirping enthusiastically—about what, I couldn't be sure. I realized that I knew blessed little about what was around me. I had shaped my home environment to my own preferences for order and symmetry, without a thought what else might be possible. And now I was at a loss even to say where those preferences of mine had even come from.

As my foot got better, I started walking around the yard, careful with my steps so as not to crush anything. I wended my way through the overgrown lawn to the flower bed, where the hosta were still holding their own. The roses indeed needed pruning. My responsibility, I guess, was to keep them under control so they didn't create an unwelcome thicket of thorns that crowded everything else out. It was a duty to the yard, I felt.

And the colours had changed. Yes, the roses would bloom in their normal way, but there were no geraniums or impatiens. Wildflowers had taken over, especially a tall, daisy-like flower with lavender petals. I later found out that this was fleabane, which apparently grows just about everywhere. I hadn't ever noticed any before. It was quite pretty.

I will let nature take its course this year—except for the roses. But I am not sure what I will do for next year. A balance must be struck. This I now understand. But I shall have to figure out where that balance lies. In the meantime, I savour the arrival of the unexpected.

TRASH DAY

Timothy Niedermann

It was Trash Day, the town's annual spring street clean-up effort. Shelley and Kate's assigned route was a couple of kilometres on a quiet road lined with maples, beech and oak, with houses spaced far apart. Each woman carried a bag for trash and a bag for recyclables. Kate was wearing surgical gloves. Shelley wasn't as particular.

The two hadn't seen each other for a while, so this was a nice chance for them to catch up. They walked slowly as they chatted.

Shelley was her usual bouncy self. "Sure is a great day for a walk! Sun's out, not too hot or humid."

Kate nodded.

Shelley went on. "Besides, we're being useful. I actually do this on my walks all year long."

"Pick up trash?"

"Not trash. Returnables. The bottles and cans you get money for when you return them. Except that I just take what I find to the town's recycling centre. Doing my part to help keep taxes low."

"At five cents a pop?"

"Well, things add up."

They filled each other in on their families—kids sports and university aspirations, Shelley talked about her husband Jack, while Kate, who was divorced, had to admit that the dating scene was quiet. Shelley, a part-time teacher, was nearing the end of the school year. Kate, an accountant, was recovering from tax season.

Shelley was beginning to talk about summer plans when she stopped in mid-sentence.

"Oh, look! What have we here? Our first returnable. A Labatt's Blue Light. The high schooler's tipple of choice. In my day anyway."

Shelley tossed the can into her sack then shook her head, smiling.

"You know, I have a theory."

"What's that?"

"I'd like to think that most of this stuff, the litter I mean, is coming from teenagers, kids cruising around flexing their adolescent irresponsibility. You, know, the beer cans, the gum wrappers, the cigarette butts. It's the age. High school. Experimenting. Getting a greater sense of freedom. Learning to drive. Hormones! Chucking their empty cans and what not out of the car before they get home, so mom and dad are none the wiser. Teenage thoughtlessness. But the nice thing is that it's just a phase. They'll grow out of it." She paused. "Eventually."

They both laugh.

A car came toward them, slowing down as it approached. Just as it passed by, its driver's window opened, and a glowing cigarette butt flew out.

Both Kate and Shelley raised their middle fingers in the car's direction as it accelerated down the road.

"Shit! What sort of idiot still smokes?" Kate went over and crushed the butt with her shoe, then bent over and picked it up with two blue-covered fingers and dropped it into her trash bag.

Kate gave Shelley a look.

"He didn't look like a teenager."

Shelley replied brightly, "The exception that proves the rule!"

They both laughed.

They continued to walk from driveway to driveway, picking up a soda can here, a used tissue there and some odd things: a bottle-shaped dog toy that squeaked, a bicycle pump, a Blue Jays cap. Shelley inspected the cap, and, finding that it was fairly clean, rolled it up and put it in her pocket.

"Go Jays!" she said with a grin.

As she said that, Shelly leaned down to pick up a candy wrapper. When she stood up, she noticed a dark look on Kate's face.

"What's wrong?"

Kate waited a moment before replying. "I had a fight with my boss yesterday."

"Jesus, that's not good! What about?"

"Well, we have recycling bins in our office kitchen and lunchroom where we can throw bottles and cans. I was working late a few days ago and was in the lunchroom when the cleaning woman came in and started dumping the stuff in the recycling bins in with the rest of the trash."

"Oh, for God's sake!"

"Yeah. I asked her why, and you know what she said? She said that's what her instructions were."

"You're kidding!"

"Wish I were. Anyway, the next day I went to see my boss. I told him what I had seen, and he just looked at me and said, 'And?' What a piece of work! I mean, the whole office had wanted to do recycling, and the managers had been supportive."

Kate's voice rose as she went on.

"Then he starts lecturing me: 'Why should we pay extra for a recycling service when it's just going to be shipped out and dumped in the ocean? It's cheaper all around just to send it to the landfill.' I tried to say something, but he interrupted me. 'Look, if you want to take responsibility for taking out the recycling, fine. Just don't ask me to pay for it.' And then he just put his head down and went back to what was on his desk. So, I left."

"What an asshole!"

"It's the way he thinks. Money, money, money. But you know what really gets to me?"

"What's that?

"His self-serving, penny-pinching hypocrisy. He's just making excuses. He could easily find a reputable recycling company. There are plenty. He thinks he's better than those people who dump in the ocean because he sends it to a landfill," she said, "but they *dump* it too! Landfills *are* dumps for Christ's sake! And God knows what seeps out of them into our earth and water! He's just passing the buck and avoiding responsibility. The out-of-sight, out-of-mind mentality."

"Yeah, I know the type. Lazy. Won't make the least extra effort to do the right thing."

Shelley stopped and thought for a moment.

"You should call his bluff."

"What?"

"You could collect all those bottles and cans yourself and give them to the town so that they could redeem them."

"That's a lot of work."

"Yeah, but maybe others at your office would pitch in."

"I suppose so, but it's one more time someone has to pick up someone else's mess." She paused for a moment. "Like we're doing today, perhaps?"

Kate's tone was sardonic, but Shelley smiled and nodded energetically.

"Exactly. Picking up after our kids."

"Sometimes seems like that's all we ever do."

Shelley laughed.

"Yeah, but that's part of being a parent. At least today we're outside in the fresh air."

Kate turned her head sharply.

"Wow, see that?" she said excitedly, pointing to a paperback lying under a bush. "A Nora Roberts novel! Trash reading to be sure!" She looked at the cover then shoved the book into her recyclables sack.

"Have you ever read her?" asked Shelley.

Kate made a face. "Yes, once. A woman in my book group thought we should read her to see what all the fuss was about."

"And?"

"She tells a good enough story, but it ain't literature, as they say. Entertaining enough, but shallow. And it sure isn't Canadian. So, as penance, we read Robertson Davies's *Deptford Trilogy*."

"Ooh, you jumped right into the deep end!"

At that, Shelley walked over to the side of the road.

"Ah, what's this? White Claw hard seltzer? Who thought that one up? Looks like Labatt's has competition."

The road now curved slightly downhill with both sides now forested. Though it wasn't yet visible, the road ended at the bottom of the hill, where it intersected with one of the town's main roads, on the far side of which was a lake that served as a reservoir for the water needs of a nearby city, about twenty kilometres away.

Both sides of the road were now forested, part of the watershed for the reservoir. A stream ran parallel to their road on the right, and they could just hear the melody of its flow.

"We're nearly to the reservoir, so we're almost done."

Shelley stared up as a red-winged blackbird flew just over their heads.

"I love this part of the road. When I was a kid, we used to play Indians in the woods over there." She points to the left where an opening in the undergrowth revealed a lightly used path leading into the forest. "Not cowboys and Indians, just Indians. We made our own moccasins and even put up a tepee in our back yard to sleep in during the summer. Those were the days."

Shelley stooped down to pick up a can.

"Another White Claw! Labatt's is definitely in trouble!"

Their sacks were slowly getting full. Shelley found a tray of Tim Hortons cups and crushed them with her foot before shoving them into her sack. One was half-full and splashed on her sneaker.

"Lazy commuters. The kids have company! It's just too easy to roll down the car window and throw your shit out."

"Eww! A condom! Kate, you have the gloves."

"Gee, thanks."

Kate gingerly picked up the offensive piece of latex and dropped it into her open sack.

"Was it used?"

Kate made a face. "I didn't check."

They were approaching the intersection with the main road. Kate held up her mostly full sack.

"Not a bad haul. Nice to have our road clean for another year."

Shelley was walking toward an old, partially collapsed stone wall on the side of the road.

"One last White Claw can!"

She clambered over several fallen stones and grabbed a tall can off the top of the wall.

"Holy shit! Kate, come here!"

Kate hurried over and stood next to Shelley, who was pointing behind the wall. Lining the stream for at least twenty metres was a jumbled pile of loose cans, bottles and cardboard containers, some of which looked fresh, others in various stages of decomposition.

Shelley spread out her arms and waved excitedly. “The motherlode! This is great! How many do you think are there?”

Kate’s finger bounced up and down as she counted softly.

“There’s at least a dozen sixpacks, don’t know how many loose cans. And that’s just the top layer. There’s a lot more.”

“That’s a lot of returnables!” Shelley pulled out her phone. “I’m calling Paul to see if he can bring the pickup down here.”

Kate got down off the wall and walked toward the pile. Kneeling down at the water’s edge, she noticed something and began to push the bottles and cans aside.

“Shit!”

Underneath the bottles and cans, the bulk of the pile, really, were empty motor oil cans, plastic antifreeze bottles and other containers whose labels had peeled off over time. Some lay at the water’s edge, others sat in the stream itself. The telltale colours of a chemical film reflected from the water nearby.

As she watched, Shelley’s chipper voice extolling the returnables find to her husband behind her, Kate could see the film’s bright trail mix into the current and form a little river of its own as it flowed downstream toward the lake below. She pulled her arms around her and shuddered.

PATAGONIA

Cora Siré

I'm sitting on a low stone wall outside Hotel Llao Llao. From the top of a steep hill, the hotel overlooks Lake Nahuel Huapi. Beyond the glacial waters, the Andes jut in the distance, snow-capped and resolute. *Magnificent* doesn't come close. Lake Louise on steroids. Just what I need. I'm here to heal.

My room isn't quite ready. I take the time to imagine the past. This is what Argentina looked like many millennia ago—minus the curving driveway, the sloping lawn and the fencing alongside beds of frenetic red rosebushes.

Fifteen minutes later I'm in my room. Very small, the least expensive, but there's a double bed with a billowy white duvet and somewhat of a view sideways if you crane your neck. It's cheap for those of us converting to pesos from dollars. But there's always some price to be paid. By nightfall, my knees are as red as the roses outside and burning hot. I was wearing a hat and long-sleeved shirt while I waited outside. My mistake was the shorts.

When I return from dinner in the hotel dining room, I can't even touch the skin around my kneecaps. For cold compresses I take all the facecloths and hand towels, soak them in ice water and spend the night under a damp duvet.

My consolation is the night sky dotted with zillions of southern constellations and the white-light flashes of shooting stars. Back in Buenos Aires, my friend Charly had said, "You need some beauty to distance yourself from grief. Patagonia is the perfect place."

I limp down for breakfast, every step the equivalent of an angry wasp swarm stinging my knees. Sitting down and getting up are the worst. All around me, the hotel guests refill their plates with delicacies from the breakfast buffet. They're mostly from Brazil, given all the Portuguese. Walking is too much, so I settle on coffee, juice and croissants brought to my table by a friendly fellow who tells me he lives here for the skiing in winter. The Argentine winter, obviously—our summer. I've heard that Canadian ski teams come to train here in July and August.

Back in my room, I watch the Clinton impeachment trial on CNN, wondering about the charges of high crimes and misdemeanours. I mean, I'm in Argentina, the country that took in war criminals in the forties, the Nazi officers who taught the military here about state terror and the systematic eradication of dissent.

Early afternoon, I hobble around the property, which appears to be a peninsula overlooking not one, but two large lakes, Nahuel Huapi and Moreno. I wind up by the pool, find a shady spot and watch the Brazilians go nuts on their phones. Their currency, the *real*, is crashing. I hear them yelling numbers as they frantically call their banks or financial advisors back in Rio or São Paulo. When I later describe this scene to Charly, he'll tell me that by the end of this January 1999, the real lost over sixty percent of its value against the dollar. Now, after markets close, there's an aura of resignation as the Brazilians plunge into the pool, then treat everyone to rounds of Cuba libres.

Their largesse dredges up what I was hoping to detach myself from. Three months ago, my mother died after a long illness. While I took care of her, she spoke often of her time in Rio. How as a refugee from Estonia she'd arrived via Sweden after the war, how the Brazilians had welcomed her into their homes and invited her to their parties. It seems I can't entirely escape her past, let alone mine.

Next morning, I drive my rental car into town. The Daewoo resembles an orthopedic shoe in white. The only vehicle available at the airport when I arrived, it makes me feel highly visible as I drive alongside the lake.

The town of San Carlos de Bariloche reflects more than a hint of Bavaria in its architecture. Wood A-frames and cottages with roses growing in semi-groomed clusters out front. I park on a steep hill and hobble into a pharmacy. A person in a white lab coat examines my knees, whistling quietly. Blisters have started forming, and it's obvious the swaths of skin between mid-thigh and shin of both my legs will soon be peeling off. The pharmacist offers me aloe lotion and a giant bottle of sunscreen, SPF 80. Such a level isn't yet available in Montreal. I ask the pharmacist why so much.

"Haven't you heard? The ozone layer is gone." I'm not sure whether he means here in Patagonia or everywhere. The pharmacist tells me there have been days when people are told to keep their children indoors to limit their exposure to ultraviolet radiation.

Feeling foolish, I go into a bar and order a Quilmes beer with some pizza. Inside the bathroom, I slather my legs with aloe. When I return to the bar, I see two teenagers pointing at my car parked outside and laughing. Then they take off down the slope on their skateboards. I wonder why Charly didn't warn me about getting sunburned. When you feel foolish, it's always easier to blame someone else.

I'm able to venture out for my last day in Bariloche. I cross Nahuel Huapi on a boat full of students on their January vacations. They're all wearing shorts and tank tops, while I'm mummified in long pants, a white shirt and my straw hat. The only other person dressed like me on the boat turns out to be a student studying environmental science at La Plata, Luigi, who compliments me on my sensible attire. Luigi says that, in addition to the risks of skin cancer, the ozone depletion has affected wind patterns and rainfall, slowing the growth of ancient forests in Patagonia.

When the boat lands, we hike together through a national park. Luigi mentions that the lack of rain has stunted trees such as the *alerce*, a cousin of the redwood, and the *araucarias,* or monkey puzzle trees, a species of evergreen so old they're considered living fossils. Hunters report finding blind rabbits, and fishermen, blind salmon, caused by exposure to radiation from holes in the ozone layer. All afternoon, wandering through the paths between the stalwart trees, I'm not aware of my burning knees—or my grief.

After the boat trip, I drive over to a café recommended by the hotel. There's a German flag alongside the Argentine one over the entrance and inside, a long counter of gateaux and tortes with labels like Linzer, Sacher and the tongue-twister Schwartzwälder Kirschtorte. All around me, people are speaking German, occasionally slipping into Spanish. I take a table overlooking the white-rose garden and order coffee and a pastry. After eating, a memory emerges. My mother's last word, *love,* as she pointed to her heart then mine. When she died that night, a flash of white light exploded in her bedroom.

Outside, on the windy mountainside, the roses bob and weave.

I'm back in Patagonia, landing again in Bariloche. The airport hasn't changed much in ten years, although the country has, after economic crises and devastation. I've changed, too, having learned that healing is not a straight-line trajectory and that emergent memories can both haunt and enlighten.

I've also learned that, although the ozone layer still has a big hole over Antarctica, the UN's Montreal protocol has been implemented with most countries phasing out the ozone-depleting chemical compounds in fridges, aerosols and industrial processes. Some scientists predict that, by 2040, the hole will shrink, if not entirely, then substantially. Nevertheless, as soon as we get outside the airport, I apply sunscreen and put on a hat.

This time, I'm tagging along with Charly, who's heading north to San Martín de los Andes. I've booked a room in a small inn there, while he'll be staying outside of town to go fly-fishing with his cousins. We pick up our rental car outside the airport. Another odd vehicle, spray-painted black so you can't even discern what make it is. Charly insists on driving, says the road is treacherous at night. Before getting in the car, he opens his suitcase and takes out a knife in a leather sheath, which he attaches to his belt. "What's that for?" I ask. "You're planning to stab some fish along the way?"

"Fishful thinking." He's got his deadpan face on, the one he resorts to when joking and, I'll soon discover, when dealing with the police. His real name is Carlos, but his friends call him Charly. He prefers to speak English with me, even though he was born and raised in Buenos Aires. I suspect he might've been the only Argentine to support the British during the Falkland Islands war.

It's dusk as we head towards the highway, the traffic moving steadily until, fifteen minutes outside of town, we slow into a long lineup of cars. After inching forward for quite a while, we reach a checkpoint with three police vehicles. Officers stand on the road stopping every single car leaving town. Charly rolls down his window.

The cop tells him our headlights aren't working. Charly flicks them on and off. It looks like they're functioning by the beams cast when they're on. When Charly moves to get out of the car, the officer tells him to stay put and asks for the registration. I open the glove compartment and pull out the mottled plastic sheath left by the rental agency. Charly takes it from me and digs into his back pocket for his wallet. The knife is on his right side, next to me, and hopefully out of the police officer's view. Charly slides a bill into the plastic sheath and hands it over. The car's too dark for me to discern the denomination, but the cop sighs, returning the registration to Charly. Clearly not enough. Charly adds two more bills. "Let me take another look," the officer says, pretending to study the registration while sliding the pesos into his pocket. Later, we'll discover that the registration is expired, that it isn't even made out for the car we've rented. The policeman doesn't say anything more, just waves us through.

Charly accelerates, and we drive on at breakneck speed. He keeps slamming the steering wheel and swearing. I assume he's ashamed about the corruption in his country, so I try to diffuse his anger with comments about how underpaying police officers obliges them to make money by other means. I'd just read an article along those lines in a left-leaning newspaper in Buenos Aires. "He's only trying to feed his family." Charly doesn't buy my argument, probably because he tilts right and has this firm belief in the work ethic. Eventually, I take the conversation elsewhere, asking him about what kind of fish he'll be looking for in the rivers around San Martín. He calms down and starts talking about the trout and how he used to go to northern Argentina until the fly-fishing there dried up, first because of intermittent drought, and then because the pesticides used to grow soya and other crops seeped into the rivers to maim, even kill the trout.

By now it's pitch-black outside, and we're alone on the Road of Seven Lakes, winding through forests, rising into the hills for the occasional glimpse of an expansive lake shimmering in the starlight. Two hours after leaving Bariloche, the paved road becomes gravel, and the car swerves and skids close to a nonexistent shoulder. Now we're both tilting right. Charly stops the car, gets out and checks the tires. "Completely and utterly bald," he says, getting back in. He has to drive at fifty, max, for the remaining three hours.

It's only the next morning, when I leave the inn, that I get a sense of San Martín, smaller than Bariloche and easier to explore. It's a town with cottages, bed and breakfasts and small inns like mine, the streets sloping down to Lake Lácar, surrounded by mountains. Every cabin and house seems well tended, with fresh paint on the wood trim and flowers in boxes by the windows. Rose bushes grow alongside the roads, with bees hovering over profusions of white and pink flowers. The place was once largely a ski resort town. In recent years, lack of snow has curtailed the ski season, and San Martín has shifted into more of a summer destination. People come from Buenos Aires to escape the January heat. Yesterday I was sweltering in forty degrees plus in the city. Here it's half that and breezy.

I take the boat across the lake to a beach near an Indigenous community. In the village, I find sweaters made of Patagonia wool and all manner of intricate beading. Every encounter with the inhabitants and the Argentines vacationing here is friendly, and I start to fall in love with the area, wishing it weren't so far to get to. Later I find out there's a direct flight from Buenos Aires to nearby Junín and wonder why Charly put us through the drive last night.

Another morning, I hike up into the mountains with a group of tourists and local people. It's a steep climb through coniferous forests, past streams and waterfalls. When we get to a lookout, I have the same sense I had outside the hotel in Bariloche. This is what Argentina looked like millennia ago. When I say this to one of the guides, Maite, she laughs and points towards a mountaintop. "Yeah, but that's Chile over there."

Walking down, Maite says she has to be careful not to inadvertently guide her groups across the border. Then she talks about what's actually happening in these mountains, how fragile the ecosystems are and the duress they're under. Deforestation has caused soil erosion and landslides. Lower snowfall and rising temperatures create avalanches. The animals are confused, some nearing extinction. The lake doesn't freeze over as much. Sheep farmers have to move their flocks when drought kills the pastures. So the landscapes might appear to be unchanged, but they are not. "Many people are indifferent," she says. "So are the politicians."

But then, as if to dispel her bitterness, Maite tells the other guide to continue with the group and leads me through a winding path in the forest of pines. We come to a tumultuous stream, take off our clothes and jump in. The water is bracing. Maite wades across the rocks to a flat area under the waterfall. I join her, and we stand there, letting the water whoosh over us. It's the closest I've ever come to feeling like Eve in Eden. But I also wonder, in ten years will this waterfall even be here?

That night I'm supposed to meet Charly and his cousins in a bar on the main strip of town. I'm running late after the hike and hurry past shops and cafés. Inside the bar, I find them sitting in a booth, eating pizza and empanadas. Charly is expansive, translating some of the slangy jokes from Spanish, the humour lost in his translation. Of course, they wind up trading fishing stories and misadventures. His cousin Rubén says that, last month, he was fishing by himself on a branch of the river near Junín. When he returned to his pickup, it was stripped of tires and all its contents. "That's why I carry a knife," Charly says. I don't even try to point out that a knife would have been moot in that circumstance.

I leave the bar as soon as possible, because tomorrow is my last full day, and I don't want to miss out. In the morning, I visit the local museum and a plaza with all manner of stands selling crafts like tie-dye scarves, silver jewellery set with unfamiliar stones and pottery. I take a hike into the national park, hoping to encounter Maite again, but she's not around.

On my way back to the inn, someone hands me a pamphlet about a poetry reading happening soon. I walk over to the small structure officially known as La Pastera, but also the Che Museum, owned and operated by the National Park of Lanín.

The courtyard's already full of people sitting in a small amphitheatre facing a quadrant where wires crisscross the space. Suspended by clothespins from the wires, large sheets of construction paper hang like laundry. The colours of the construction paper, I will later realize, are the same pinks, yellows, reds and peaches of the roses of Patagonia. Pasted onto the colours, blown-up pages of poetry.

Someone hands me a glass of wine, and I stroll among the laundry, reading the poems. It's more like a poetry viewing than a reading. A guy starts playing guitar, and, in-between songs, the emcee presents a poet. No hard sell of books, no detailed intros. The poet waves, people applaud, and we go on sitting around or reading the poetry. It's probably the easiest, most angst-free poetry event I've ever attended, and I wind up chatting with all manner of poets and hangers-on. Most are in their twenties, born more than a decade after the military dictatorship, but they've lived through the economic meltdown, and their poetry reflects an ironic disavowal of the material world, power structures and social conventions.

I enter the building to discover a small exhibition on its origins. This is where Che Guevara, then a twenty-three-year-old, asthmatic med student, and his friend Alberto spent the night—one night—in a shed on their way to Chile, then north into Peru where they stopped to volunteer at a leper colony before continuing on to Colombia and Venezuela.

The place is one of a chain of Che museums Argentina has created in various towns that have some passing relevance to Che's biography. The anti-capitalist, Marxist warrior sells well, even though it's been almost six decades since Che Guevara wrote his diary during the trip on the motorbike he named La Poderosa and six years since *The Motorcycle Diaries* made a splash in cinemas.

That night in La Pastera, a second exhibit catches my attention. Thousands of small, black-and-white photos, all headshots like those in passports, are affixed to a wall, in-between placards with explanations. It's a work in progress twenty-seven years after the end of the dictatorship in Argentina—the documentation of every single person who disappeared during the military regime. Thirty thousand, if not more. The disappearance of so many young activists, students, artists and writers, along with the thousands of others who went into exile, decimated a generation, traumatized a nation and left an intellectual vacuum.

I'm standing inside an unchangeable past. Outside is the present of this February 2010, the courtyard where people are dancing and singing and drumming and reading subversive poetry from rose-coloured papers stirring in the wind.

The airport near Coyhaique is jammed with arrivals and departures, mostly flights from Santiago, with some—like mine—coming from Buenos Aires. It's February 2020 and summer-vacation time. I plow through the crowds and their bulky backpacks towards the car rental, where I'm given a pickup truck, grey and a little dented, but the tires are fine. They have to be, I'll be driving through rough terrain. But first the highway towards town, a long, undulating ribbon flanked on both sides by mountains. To the east is Argentina. To the west the sun is sinking behind the peaks into the Pacific. Coyhaique, Chile, is closer to Cape Horn than to Santiago, way farther south than both Bariloche and San Martín on the Argentine side.

I make for Patagonia Place, where I'll be staying for five days on my own. It's up a sharp incline, through a forest of fir trees and then into a wide alley of poplars that leads to a cluster of buildings on a sloping property. Rooms are in separate sheds, one shed per guest or two. Inside my shed, the windows look out over a pasture of green with the Andes visible beyond the valley. The bathroom has the best water pressure and fixtures I've ever experienced. My quarters in no way resemble the shed in San Martín where Che slept on his motorcycle journey through Patagonia.

In the morning, I make my way to the dining hall, all wood and glass with tables and chairs already occupied by other guests. It's a friendly, relaxed place, the owner, Raquel, moving between the tables, making sure everyone gets the right breakfast. Two filmmakers sit at a table next to mine, Chilean like most of the others by the sound of their Spanish. Some are here for the fly-fishing. Just as I'm finishing my eggs, a gang walks in. Eight guys, dressed in black leather, take the long table by the window. Turns out they've been riding their motorcycles down from Lima, into Bolivia, and now through Chile, where they hope to cross a pass into Argentina, the same pass some fled across after the Pinochet coup. It's the reverse of Che's journey, and I wonder whether they're even aware of this.

The bikers joke around, eat huge plates of food and study their phones. All except the one with a bushy auburn beard who crosses his arms on the table and lays his head down. I assume he's hungover, until I hear him heave a wrenching, phlegmy cough. When they're finished eating, his friends practically carry him out of the dining room.

Later I drive into town, dressed in a light toque, down jacket and jeans. It's cold for a cloudless summer day. Wisps of haze hang over the hills, a morning mist I assume, until I discern a smoky smell. Despite the environmental hazards, many still heat their stoves with wood or toxic briquets. Mountain ridges surround Coyhaique, so the smoke can't disperse and winds up compressed into a dense cloud that sits over the town's valley, causing one of the worst air-quality levels in all the Americas.

At the crossroads where I turn into town, two acrobats on unicycles are juggling with swords, deftly moving from lane to lane to avoid the cars. They're covered in tattoos, wearing bicycle shorts and undershirts. There's no receptacle for tips, and they don't come close enough to the vehicles to collect any money. It's a free show that endears me to the place and to the two of them.

I find parking outside a commercial strip with shops that look like they've been here since the Pinochet coup. I walk up and down the streets, stop at a grocery store and pick up some peaches. Few of the roads have sidewalks, but most of them have thick clusters of rosebushes alongside the pavement. All tangly, a little dusty, some of them climbing up the low stone walls and overhanging from gates with peeling paint.

In the town plaza, backpackers congregate on benches alongside dancers, hula hoop gyrators and buskers with guitars or Andean flutes known as *quenas*. Here and there a table of wares much like the crafts I'd spotted in San Martín ten years ago. I'd like to linger, but I'm supposed to meet up with someone called Ernesto in a café set back in an alley without a street number or name.

When I finally find the place, there's only one adult occupying a table, along with four children, ranging in age from about two to eight. I ask if he's Ernesto, and he nods yes, as serious as his name implies, and I wonder if he knows that Che's first name was, in fact, Ernesto. This Ernesto has Che's furrowed brow and thick eyebrows and a similar intense expression. The kids check me out, and Ernesto's embarrassed enough to mumble something about them never having met a Canadian before. He's drinking coffee, and the place doesn't have much else that would appeal to kids, so I open the bag of peaches, and soon their faces are dripping with juice.

He asks after Charly, who came here to fly-fish a few years ago. I tell him Charly's busy with work, something to do with currency exchange and shifting dollars to and from pesos. When I saw Charly last week in Buenos Aires, his knee jiggled, and he looked exhausted. He said he'd met with a honcho in the currency-trading business the day before, a guy who, when people come to see him in his office, places a pistol on his desk. Charly said it works for keeping the meetings really short. We were at El Cuartito, an iconic pizza place where construction workers eat alongside oligarchs in pressed linen suits and silk ties. Ramón, the waiter, knows Charly so well he doesn't have to order. Ramón automatically brings him his two squares of *napoletana* and a glass of Quilmes. This time, when the waiter brought the order, Charly deadpanned, "I didn't order this." Ramón punched him on the shoulder and grinned. While eating, Charly urged me to visit Chile, specifically the Patagonian town of Coyhaique. Later I walked around the pizzeria, taking in vintage boxing posters and the framed blue-and-white No. 14 jersey: *Para El Cuartito con todo mi cariño—Maradona, 2016.* When I came back to the table, Charly said he'd checked in with Ernesto, who was available to guide me.

Ernesto takes out a handkerchief from his pocket and cleans the kids' faces and hands. I wonder if they'll be coming along on our excursion, but I don't want to ask. When he's done with the handkerchief, Ernesto tells me he'll pick me up at Patagonia Place tomorrow, eight a.m. sharp. "I'll come alone, don't worry." Now I'm wondering how much Ernesto will charge me, and before I can ask, he says, "How does fourteen thousand pesos sound? That includes lunch." I'm still struggling with the Chilean currency conversion, which I'd memorized as "take off two zeros and divide by six." Maybe it's the altitude or smoke inhalation, but my brain's not up to the task, so I try to casually take out my phone and do the calculation, which comes out to twenty-three dollars Canadian. Ernesto gets the kids ready, and I nod. "Sounds good." He doesn't say much more, and his children file out the door behind him.

I finish my coffee alone in the café except for the owner, who studies his phone behind the counter to music coming from the plaza through the open windows. This café is like most of the venues in Coyhaique. It sells coffee and nothing else. No adornments or fancy decorations. There's an authenticity to the place that I appreciate. The people, too, like Ernesto, don't bother with pretence or fakery. Maybe that's why Charly sent me here, in addition to the promise of great beauty.

It's almost noon, and the sun has warmed things up. I tie my jacket around my waist and look for a place that sells maps of the area. Charly told me my cellphone might be out of range when I go into the bush with Ernesto, and I always like to know where I am and the names of the lakes and mountains, their relative geographic position. On the street where I parked, people are nailing plywood to the windows. Inside an outfitter shop, I find a map and ask about the plywood. A precaution, I'm told. There's a protest march tonight.

When I ask what for, the guy says, "Everything. Schools, housing, health care."

That night in my shed, I feverishly search for details on the protest in Coyhaique but find nothing on-line. Then I start looking up Chile's history, read Allende's last radio speech from the Presidential palace during the 1973 coup and find his address to the UN a year earlier.

In front of a packed assembly in New York, Allende denounced the multinational corporations who were acting against public interests and in violation of elected representation. It was as if Allende was defending the environment when he called out the international economic exploitation as another manifestation of imperialism—one that is "more cunning and terrifyingly effective." The Chilean president received a standing ovation. Less than a year later, Allende died as Pinochet carried out his coup on September 11, 1973.

Next morning, I'm up early and make my way to the breakfast place in the dazzling light. There's that smoky smell, but the sky is an intense blue that should have its own name, like "Andean celeste." Raquel brings me a pot of coffee and some warm milk. "Your eye looks red," she says, adding that there's a nasty virus circulating among some of her guests. I do have a scratchy throat, but I hadn't noticed anything wrong with my eye when I showered in the bathroom. Maybe because the mirror was steamed up. The bikers come in to occupy their table. The guy with the bushy auburn beard isn't among them. They sit down and two of them start coughing. Raquel goes over to take their order.

At exactly eight, Ernesto pulls up outside the window. He's hauling a green boat on a trailer hitched to the pickup. I didn't know we'd be going for a boat ride. Raquel brings him a coffee while I go to my shed for my backpack and hat. My eye does look red, but it doesn't hurt. When I return to the breakfast place, Ernesto goes to the bathroom. Raquel says, "You're in good hands. Ernesto's a very good guide. Only problem, he doesn't speak much. Some visitors have had issues communicating." When he comes back, Raquel tells him to stop at a pharmacy so I can get some eye drops. We do that on the way to the national park. Since my wallet is out, I pay Ernesto for the excursion, and he buys two asthma inhalers for his kids. I get lozenges for my throat and what I'm told is a bottle of aspirin-like pills.

Ernesto steers the pickup south into the hills. He smiles when I unfold my map. "That's my job." I study the map and then his profile for insights into what kind of person he is, considering we'll be spending the day together, and he's not much of a talker. I have to pick up on the non-verbal cues. Ernesto looks to be about thirty, meaning he grew up after the end of Pinochet's dictatorship. He's wearing jeans and a jacket over a down vest and T-shirt, hiking boots on his feet. The interior of the pickup is immaculate. I decide to ask him about the protest. "Did you go there last night?" He shakes his head. "We put our five kids to bed, including the baby you didn't meet yesterday. Then I made your lunch." Nothing about the struggle, or purpose of the protest.

We drive the long strip of a highway. After a while, it's as if the mountains are moving towards us, and, sure enough, when they're closer, Ernesto turns onto a dirt road, and we jolt along for several hilly kilometres. Up a precipice from where a huge lake is visible, the crystalline blues of the water as intense as the sky, then down towards a beach where he backs the trailer up onto a ramp. When we stop, I jump down and go to the back to help unload the boat. Ernesto's already slid the vessel out and it lands on the ramp with a wooden crunch. The green boat sports its name in yellow paint, *Hasta la victoria siempre*. By the time I've taken that in, Ernesto is back in the truck and drives to a parking spot above the beach. There's no one else out this early, and the lake is empty of any other boats or people. But my impression of emptiness is an illusion. When we return in the late afternoon, the beach will be crowded and the parking lot full.

Ernesto hands me a life jacket. I ask about the boat's name. He says it was there when he bought the boat. He's pushing the vessel down the ramp before I can ask whether he knows that the phrase is lifted from Che's farewell letter to Castro, written in 1965, when the warrior left Cuba for the Congo and later Bolivia.

The boat glides into the water butt out so I can step in without getting my feet wet. I sit in the middle next to the cooler. Ernesto gets in, takes an oar to push the boat completely into the lake, and starts the outboard motor. Three pulls and we're off, the motor's thrum not deafening but not quiet enough to allow for conversation.

I swivel around to face where we're heading. The boat isn't leaky, but the wind from our speed pushes my hat back, so I have to jam it low on my forehead. There's no cell reception. I slide my phone into my backpack, find my tube of sunscreen and slather my face and hands. I'm feeling twitchy, so I take an aspirin, unaware that the next day I will develop a wicked cough that accompanies me on four flights (Santiago to Lima to Orlando to Montreal) alongside many passengers who are also coughing that February 2020 in what will, at first, seem an inexplicably bizarre coincidence. I also do not know that I'll never see Charly again, after he succumbs to the virus at a hospital in Buenos Aires.

It's a long drive across the centre of Lake Paloma until a waterway connects us to a second lake, Azul. Here the water is more emerald than turquoise, more milky than crystalline. In the park, there's even a third lake, El Desierto, but we never make it that far.

On one side of Lake Azul, the mountain rises almost vertically. The occasional waterfall sprays down between the pine trees. Past the tree line are triangulating glaciers and sheer rocky precipices. The other side of the lake has a gentler slope with meadows, and I can discern the occasional cottage perched on a hill. But there are no other signs of human existence, and it's tempting to fall for the illusion that this landscape looks exactly like it did millennia ago, carved by the ice age, flooded by the glacier melt. How can I really know that? I reach down to put my hand in the water. The boat tilts, and I feel the numbing iciness of the lake. But the water is actually warmer than it once was, the air impure, the unseeable wildlife in distress. Twenty years ago, I first came to Patagonia for healing, when, all along, it's Patagonia that needs to be healed.

The hours of constant motorized thrumming, the choppy waters that have the boat bucking rhythmically off the waves, and the largesse of the landscapes and how they seem to transcend time make for a hypnotic mindset. Allende's words tickertape in my head. Frontal attack. Global interests. No controls.

What if Allende's message had been heeded back in the seventies? What if nations had understood the harm being caused by rampant globalized industrialization and trade and moved swiftly to regulate the multinationals? The massive deforestation of Chile that occurred under Pinochet, the privatization of water management to the benefit of mines and corporate interests might have been avoided.

Allende closed his UN address by declaring his certainty that human values can never be destroyed. Echoing Che's infamous phrase, "Ever onward to victory," it was Allende's nod to the future. An hypothesis still being tested half a century later, I'm thinking, when I hear a piercing whistle. I turn around to look at Ernesto, and he points to the cooler and then at some trees in the distance. I nod, and he starts steering left towards the shore.

Just as I'm wondering whether I'll have to scramble up a sheer rock face once we arrive, Ernesto pulls into a bay with a rocky beach where we soon land for lunch. He unpacks the cooler, laying containers of food on a blanket covering the stones. While Ernesto uncorks a bottle of wine, I go looking for a hidden spot to pee. Ernesto carefully keeps his back to me.

On my way back to the beach I come upon an unruly, waist-high wall of resilience: Patagonia roses in bushy clusters of red, pink, yellow and white that someone might once have tended but has since abandoned.

TIO

Matthew Murphy

In the tunnels of the mountain, Tio reigns supreme. He emerges in the dusty glare of the headlamp, arms grasping, face scowling, his diabolic features a dim and devilish red, festooned with the offerings of the miners—a necklace of desiccated coca leaves and tobacco, a cigarette jutting from his mouth having been placed by a miner days ago, holding sway over the convictions of many of those who chip away at the tunnel walls hoping for a lode of tin, a vein of silver—whatever the mountain chooses to yield, if anything.

Pablo stood in front of the moody, malevolent statue, revealed in the almost palpable blackness in a semi-silhouette cast by the cone of his headlamp, and he regarded the subterranean god of the miners with muted reverence and humility to pay his respects. He and Juanita were hoping for another baby, though at this late point in Juanita's life that hope was waning. He opened the little plastic bottle of nearly two-hundred proof cane alcohol that he was carrying and poured an offering onto the protruding penis of the seated statue, following this single-sip sacrifice with a sip of his own—a burning, numbing shot of liquor down his throat into the awaiting cauldron of his belly. It had the fumy, poisonous aftertaste of nearly pure alcohol. After his sip, he lit a freshly rolled cigarette, spiced with herbs to negate the effects of the tobacco, and smoked in silence before beginning his shift.

Outside the mine, it was still dark, though the gathering light of the predawn, and even midnight itself, were nothing compared to the eternal midnight opacity of the tunnels. A blind world hewn from the rock over centuries. The rocks had resounded and absorbed the hollering of men, the shunting squealing trundle of ore carts, the crunching concussion of dynamite, the chink of picks and shovels and of hammers hammering in the bolted wooden frames they had hoped would hold the mountain up over their heads. It had resounded and absorbed the lashing of whips, the scream and whimper and plaintive prayer of African and Indian slaves and the bullying shouts of their drivers. The mud below had absorbed and slaked its thirst on their sweat and their blood, and whatever painted or earthen evocation of Tio that had stood or sat and leered in the tunnels at any one time had done so impassively, with hopeful offerings adorning his form or strewn about his feet in tribute. In these catacombs, there were ghosts. Unabsorbed by the rocks, seemingly unreceived by any greater eternity, from time to time they moaned—or was it just the wind?

His cigarette finished, Pablo stuffed his cheeks with a plug of coca leaves to mitigate the altitude and began sloshing his way through the mucky puddles farther into the mine, his pick slung over his shoulder as though it were a rifle and he a soldier. The rock walls dripped and trickled with water, making soft music with every falling drop. He thought to himself how nice that today would be a relatively quiet one in the tunnels. Not too much clamour. He had done very poorly lately. His stope had yielded little of any value to the markets. But there was still tin in the mountain and, even after the great Spanish imperial thirst for treasure, silver. So, he had been able to mine just enough to feed his growing family over the last eighteen years, as well as hire an apprentice. Occasionally he was even able to purchase new tools, such as an automatic winch to pull his ore up from the bowels of the mountain rather than haul it up by hand crank with aching and burning biceps as he had for many years.

After a few minutes, he shimmied his way up through a tunnel barely wide enough for his body, climbing and grasping hold and stepping on protrusions of rock to hoist himself upward to his level. Then he crawled along a low-hanging tunnel over blasted gravel to his own stope, his own share in the cooperative mines of Cerro Rico in Bolivia.

Potosi awoke slowly, as always it did, the fingers of the rising sun reading a pointed Braille of old steeples, of spires, of convents and cobblestones and the deep ruts of old alleys, of chips and holes and tiles and cracks and stucco. Interpreting the city's history in its rose-coloured hue, the ghost-light of blood long ago shed—and the possibility of a better life over the mountains.

The streets of the old city were nearly empty this morning. A puff of breeze, the awakening breath of day. The rasp of debris blowing across the cobblestones of the central plaza.

Laughter and footsteps, a chorus of awakening voices speaking English. A handful of travellers made their way through the central plaza into the near-empty alleyways overlooked by the façades of colonial churches and tenements.

"Which agency is it again?" asked one male voice in a mild Dutch accent.

"I don't know," replied another voice, this one female with a refined English accent. "But I think it is the one with the mannequin of a miner in a rubber suit. Is it not, Rhonda?"

"It most certainly is," answered Rhonda in a clipped English-Canadian accent.

An old Quechua woman shuffled by over the cobbles, hunched over a gnarled cane, draped in a ratty blue poncho and skirt, the black braids hanging under her bowler hat swinging with each swaying, uncertain step. She put out her hand to beg, her scrunched paper-bag face sad and whiskered and prematurely aged, her jaw grinding side to side which accentuated her sunken cheeks, her toothless appearance. Her hand jittered.

"Oh, my," said the English woman, taken aback at the sight. "Perhaps I should give her something?"

"Perhaps you should, Sally, talking about her as you are in the third person as if she's not there," chided the Dutchman. Sally responded by rummaging through her jean pockets for change, coming up with a few pesos, which she placed in the woman's expectant palm.

"*Gracias,*" she said in a small, diffident voice.

"*Quisiera una foto, por favor?*" asked Rhonda. Then, to the others: "I feel maybe we purchased the right." Sally and the Dutchman looked about awkwardly.

"*Si,*" was the tired, reluctant answer. "*Si.*" Granted license, Rhonda took aim with the camera slung about her neck. The woman looked stunned, caught as she was in the camera's crosshairs. With the click of a button her discomfort was immortalized. The woman shuffled onwards, jaw grinding, hands quivering.

"Good God, Rhonda, that was just tactless," Sally said laughing. "Absolutely tactless."

In the darkness beyond, the thump and shudder of a dynamite charge. Pablo spat a greenish wad of coca leaf and saliva into the gravel and dust at his feet. Wadded between his gums and cheek, the remaining bolus of coca leaves gradually numbed the side of his mouth, its sweetish, resinous flavour strong on his tingly tongue. He stood leaning on his pickaxe, holding its metal head like the crook of a cane, anger rising. He felt a tickle deep in his chest, and proceeded to cough, a parched and dusty hacking cough, a small puff of white dust erupting from his mouth as he did so. Twenty years. Twenty years he had been in this mine, and his lungs were finally giving way under the weighted accumulation of dust that eventually had its way with its steady and persistent erosion, the dust that eventually sanded and scoured the miners out of existence, that caused them to die in spasms of heaving coughs, more often than not in a state of penury. But that was not the source of any but an immediate irritation. What really peeved him right now was that Arturo was late.

He muttered a curse and continued chipping away at the rock wall, the stones still trickling water and making soft music with every falling drop. He chipped and he hacked. Nothing. Tio in his caprice was not yielding.

From behind he heard the sounds of exertion, of huffing and puffing and of a slide of gravel giving way. He turned and saw Arturo lowering himself from the hole of the tunnel into the chamber of the stope, the cone of his headlamp illuminating piles of gravel and jumbles of rocks as though they were cairns piled in honour of the fallen in a Valhallan hall of heroes.

"Arturo, you're late! What the hell is the matter with you? You want to stay with me, you show up on time!" Another cough, another puff of chalky white dust.

Arturo, a boy of sixteen, was prepared for this greeting. "Sorry!" he shouted as he adjusted his hard hat, which had slid to the side as he had lowered himself from the tunnel mouth.

"You must show up on time! I have been here now a half hour hacking away at this damn rock with no result! I would have almost twice as much done if you had showed up when you were supposed to get here. Do you understand?"

"Yes, yes, I am sorry!" Arturo felt his legs go bandy and rubbery under the barrage of Pablo's scolding. "I am sorry." Shamed, he averted his eyes from the stern expression of Pablo's deeply creased and lined face. If Pablo smelled the liquor on his breath he would surely fire him. That he made it here after such a long night's celebration was amazing, a long night of carousing in honour of his cousin's birthday that ended perilously close to the witching hour of awakening for another endless day of night in the mine. Another day of likely fruitless toil. How his head ached, how he wished he were a slug so he could slither under a rock in the blackness and hide from the responsibilities that beckoned in the unwelcome handle of his pick, in the cumbersome apparatus of the air drill.

"I was there for a while, and I still managed to get here," Pablo reminded him. "Had you been here, we might have hit something worth . . . worth doing all this digging for." Another dusty cough.

"Yes, yes, I am sorry. I will get to work now." Arturo's head still hung in shame and in expectation of further wrath. This was duly delivered in the form of a cuff across his cheek, which knocked off his hard hat and left him stinging and smarting and sent him scuttling for his helmet and his tools. Chastened, he set about expiating his sins through work, chipping away at the rock wall, chipping away into the frozen magma, the parsimonious tide of rock that is Cerro Rico.

The tourists made their way in a cluttered van up a gravel road along the slopes of Cerro Rico clad in yellow rubber waders, rubber boots, heavy jackets, and hard hats equipped with battery-operated lamps, along with their guide Mario, a former miner himself, and the sleepy driver who smoked the whole way.

The mountain itself was quite ugly, having long been stripped of its surface, reduced to a giant dun-coloured heap of gravel honeycombed with tunnel entrances, much like a giant anthill. They wound their way along the edge of the slope, overlooking Potosi in the valley below, alongside an assortment of tin-roofed shacks and garbage hovels hugging the rubble-strewn embankments of the mountainside.

". . . and the miners routinely die of silicosis after ten to fifteen years," Mario continued explaining in a subtle Spanish-flavoured accent. "Me, I was tested for it after I left and got away okay."

"How did you get out of the mines?" asked Jan, rapt with attention at all the details, both aural and visual, that filled his perceptions: the ramshackle sheds, the gravel mountains, the roving history lesson on the cooperative mines. His friends back in Appledoorn would never believe any of this, the surreality of it all, from the scenery, from the stories he was hearing, from the sticks of dynamite they had purchased from the miners' market at the base of the mountain in the streets of Potosi, an open-air bazaar hawking all the wares catering to the needs of the miners—explosives, safety equipment, totems and talismans, coca, herbal cigarettes—as chickens skittered and pecked in the alleys, giving the market a slightly voodoo atmosphere to Jan's impressionable sensibilities.

"I met my wife here," said Mario. "She is from Australia. She was studying here, and I met her and married her, and when I am back in town, I sometimes lead tours for some extra money or even go back into the mine to help my brothers. I send them money, so they have good equipment. A couple of them have gotten pretty successful on their own, you know." Mario looked at the three travellers in his charge, watching them look out the windows in disbelief, noting the blonde British girl in particular as she awkwardly adjusted her mouth to accommodate a wad of coca, her tongue poking and bulging about here and there as it shepherded errant leaves back to their pen between gum and cheek.

"How do you like the coca?"

"Oh, great," she said with an unconvincing smile. She looked nauseous.

"Many foreigners don't like it. Me, I love it!" Laughter. "Keeps away the altitude sickness, you know? All the miners here, they need it. This is the highest mine in the world: over forty-two hundred metres above sea level."

Jan whistled through his teeth. Rhonda snapped a picture through the streaked and smudgy van window. Sally continued tonguing the coca leaves in her mouth, her mouth twisting and contorting sourly this way and that, looking uneasy about what they were about to do, where they were about to go.

"It's pretty good, actually," said Rhonda. "Takes some getting used to, but y'know . . . it's got its own flavour. An interesting flavour. Very . . . ." Her voice trailed.

"Resinous," Sally said with a definitive precision. "Very resinous, very *green*. And"—she leaned forward and spat the sodden green gob of coca leaves into a tissue in her hand—"very gross." A chorus of laughter all around.

"Me, I like it," said Jan, ruminating on its flavour. "I agree, Sally, it is very resinous. But it is also sort of sweet—maybe a bit much at first, but still sweet and, well, sweet, I guess. Any thoughts, Rhonda?"

"I think it's neat. It tastes a lot like you think leaves would taste."

“Do you think it tastes like cocaine?” asked Jan to all in the cluttered and dusty van, bumping and winding its way up the mountain road. “I wouldn’t know, of course. I am not sure about the rest of you though.” An impish grin.

“Umm,” said Sally, matching Jan’s grin. “All I can say is, who’s perfect?”

Mario was laughing quietly to himself during this conversation. When he was their age, at this time of day on most days, he was toiling in the mine. Every time he took this drive up the mountain, he was stirred by memories of making his way up the slopes in the darkness and keeping at the edge of his consciousness the grim knowledge that he was about to be at it again, exhausting himself in the darkness in dull drudgery, the endless hours punctuated by moments of fear and small instances of humour. His hands, once nimble with pencil and paint brush, were now shaky and nearly numb. If only these kids knew.

“See these huts, here?” he asked, gesturing to a shanty just below a clearing on the slope. “Women stay in those, and they sort through ore by hand and smelt what they can with hand tools before it goes off to the hot smelter. They don’t make much, of course, but it’s better than nothing.” This story never failed to shock, and he was ruefully rewarded by the bulging eyes and incredulous expressions of the three tourists.

The van stopped in the clearing.

“And here we are,” Mario said, sliding open the van door and letting in the dusty air. “Get all of your stuff, make sure you’ve got everything. Don’t forget your gifts for the miners—that keeps them liking tourists! And don’t forget the dynamite.”

Out they stumbled, onto the dusty mountainside. Junk was strewn all about; cast-off bits of scrap, rusty odds and ends, bottles, cans, cigarette butts. Below, Potosi huddled in the valley, its blocks a-jumble, its steeples rising above in elegance, sharpening into fine points in stylized imitation of the mountain summits surrounding them. The group followed Mario along a rusty metal railroad to the mouth of a tunnel trussed in a bolted wooden framework. Beyond was an inky darkness.

"And in we go!" shouted Mario with a flourish.

In the dripping darkness of the tunnel, the steel rails of the ore-cart track vanished into solid blackness. The solidity of the darkness startled and intimidated each of them. It became quite apparent to them that they were in a dangerous place, and as they sloshed forward through mucky puddles, the light behind them faded and eventually vanished, locking them in a semblance of endless night, the sound of trickling water in the darkness adding to the sense of unease.

Damn him! thought Pablo as Arturo dropped his pick and tripped over a fallen rock. "Be more careful, will you? Get to your senses, already! You know, as they say, 'Time is money!' You must make me rich, Arturo, you must make me rich because, me"—he coughed a dry, dusty cough for emphasis—"I have little of either. Pick up your tool and get working."

"Yes, Uncle, yes. I am sorry." Arturo pulled himself up from the stones and uttered a small cough of his own. He felt a slight chill in his spine. Perhaps this was incipient silicosis. He had been at work in the mine for several years now, and surely his turn would come as it had to so many others, as it had to Pablo, coughing and hacking and sputtering his days away. Arturo picked up his pickaxe and took a sip from his water bottle, his head still thudding out the last of his hangover. "I will get working again."

"Yes, enough talking already and more working." Pablo was aware of the irony of this statement, uttering a thin-lipped grin on his lined, sandpaper face, and he even whistled a couple of random notes, having warmed to his workday, and having a little fun with Arturo's sense of guilt and shame over coming into work late, as if he himself had never done so in his youth about every other week. "Get moving, you, if you ever want to be your own boss around here!"

Arturo chipped at the wall, and a slate of rock slid away with a dry squeal of stone on stone and fell to the tunnel floor with a crunch. He looked to see what riches he had brought to half light—and discovered nothing. A sigh. He hacked away again and again, looking for the gleam of silver, or at least the dull shine of tin in the cone of his headlamp. He hacked and hacked, his biceps burning as he did so, consuming himself in the rhythm of his work, thinking of nothing as he became hypnotized by the repetitive swing of his hammer, the exertion of his arms. Swing by swing the mountain gave way, a reluctant chip here, a generous slab there under the weight of Arturo's and Pablo's pickaxes. They found equilibrium in what they did, swinging back and forth like pendulums, like hypnotists' pendants, marking time, becoming time in the motion of each swing for minutes on end, grunting and sweating, before making for their water bottles and replenishing the sweat that soaked into their work clothes, while coughing and clearing their throats of the mephitic atmosphere of the mine.

On one of these water breaks, both were silent. Arturo lit up an herbal cigarette and thought of *almuerzo*. This afternoon he would hopefully enjoy chicken and soup and avocado, and he could already feel bodily cravings for food, his stomach growling and boiling in anticipation. Hunger began consuming him. He needed more smoke and more coca to suppress it. The bread and the orange he had had for breakfast were wearing off fast. As he puffed on his cigarette, he dreamed up big savoury meals, like steaming coils of spaghetti and tangy red Bolognese sauce with meatballs such as he saw wealthy people eating through restaurant windows in the old city streets at night. He longed for *salteñas* filled with peas and minced meat and spicy chili sauce. He craved pizza topped with pepperoni; he yearned for grilled llama, the tang of *aji* peppers. Then, for dessert—oh, dessert!—he wished for chocolate cake, and he fantasized about its moist and spongy texture, its sweetness and the creamy layer of chocolate icing basted on top like fresh stucco. Oh yes! He was so hungry he was salivating, his body was primed to eat his very thoughts, to digest from them the essence of what scant nutrients there were in them to be taken. Visions of food were conjured in the curls of cigarette smoke that drifted into the darkness.

As he took a pull from his water bottle, he thought about his future. If only he could strike a lode of silver in here and get the hell out. Get out of Potosi, and if possible, get out of Bolivia altogether. Get onto a bus and head off somewhere else, into the hills, along the Altiplano, through all the Quechua villages where he had aunts and uncles and cousins, some who trickled into the city to work in the mines, much like himself; and on and on down into the lowlands, down to Santa Cruz to take a plane out of here. He fantasized about this many times. He longed to see America, where all the movies he watched when he could watch them came from. The ones he liked, anyway. The last time he snuck into a theatre, he saw *Smokin' Aces*. Now there was a movie. Gangsters living the kind of gangster life he fantasized about, if only to get out of the drudgery of the mines. Beautiful women. Guns and action. Most of all, lots of money. Much more money than he would ever mine out of the reluctant rock of Cerro Rico, of that he was sure.

Two years earlier, his brother Marco had been killed in a mine cave-in, and his sister Tica had died in childbirth. And last year his father had died of a heart attack, though it surely had something to do with his compounded grief and his own case of silicosis. He was wracked with spasms of wet and hacking coughs for the past several years, and the two deaths in the space of three months rapidly worsened his condition. In his final months he was a little blue in the face, not that it would make him stop smoking. In fact, he smoked more, as if to help himself on his way, and he also began drinking heavily. Arturo joked darkly with him, saying that if he was not careful, the booze would mix with the dust in one of his coughing fits and his lungs would fill with cement and harden. His mother and his other three siblings did what they could for him, all the while knowing the end was nigh.

None of these thoughts kept him from whistling as he worked, which he began after the last of his headache subsided and he had finished his cigarette. He got back to picking away at the rock walls in search of a silver vein in the flow of which he hoped to be carried away to the promise of his dreams.

The tourists made their way through the blackness along the cart tracks, feeling their way in the darkness, their feeble lamps lighting the way with jerky movements as though they were fireflies adrift in an immensity of night. They nervously listened for the trundle of a cart, but there was little activity today, which added to the haunted atmosphere, the tunnel pregnant with possible disaster.

"Come this way," said Mario. "I know where we are going. Quiet today, no?"

"It certainly is," agreed Jan. "Is it usually this quiet?"

"No, usually it is clamorous. It is just a quiet day, that's all. It's up and down, like the markets. Now—look to the right."

As they looked to the right, they saw in an alcove, wreathed in offerings, the devilish statue of Tio, naked and painted red, sitting with an erect phallus pointing toward the roof of the cavern. From his perch, Tio seemed to glower over his subterranean kingdom with livid dominion, as though dispensing justice with the magnanimous authority of the magma beneath his feet. Jan was startled. Rhonda gasped. Sally giggled, albeit nervously.

"And here he is. Tio," Mario gestured toward Tio with a flourish. "Above is Jesus's world. Down here, all belongs to Tio. Come!" He waved his arm, and they followed him closer to the statue.

"Would you like to leave an offering?" asked Mario. "See all about you, all the things the miners have left. Every Friday, there is a celebration in here. A lot of offerings are made."

Jan shrugged and said, "Why not? How about some coca leaves?"

"That would be perfect."

Jan stooped to lay some coca leaves on ground in front of the feet of the idol. Rhonda and Sally did likewise.

"Would anyone like to have a drink with me?" asked Mario.

"It's a bit early," Sally said. "But hey, why not."

"Hey, when in Rome, right?" added Rhonda.

"Now, we give a little to Tio and take a little for ourselves. Understand? You make a wish, and depending what you wish for, you pour a little on a part of his body. If you pray for wisdom, you pour some on his head. If you pray for strength, you pour some on his shoulders. If you pray for fertility," Mario suggested with a smile, "then you pour a little on his *pistole*. What do you think?"

"Well, how about wisdom?" asked Sally.

"To each their own," retorted Jan. "I'm drinking to fertility. And you, Rhonda?"

"Oh, I don't know. Strength, maybe?"

Mario opened a small plastic bottle procured from the miners' market, releasing a volatile waft of alcohol. It was almost overbearing, the reek of a wino's kiss. Each splashed a little on the body part of choice and took a small sip, shuddering as the alcohol assaulted their taste buds. Jan winced as he swallowed the liquor, and he could see Sally's face twist up on itself in disgust. Rhonda stuck her tongue out and panted out the fumy, poisonous flavour.

"Delicious, yes?" asked Mario, and he uttered a hearty laugh. "The miners drink this every day. And they drink a lot of it on Fridays, right here with Tio."

The tour group then proceeded to photograph the statue, posing with it, pretending to be scared, giving Tio the high five, leaning in for a kiss. The flash of Rhonda's camera bathed the cavern in a flickery wash of false daylight.

Sally looked about the cavern and the idol littered in desiccated offerings, at the ferocious and intimidating glare. It took her back to Eastern Turkey, to the mountaintop tomb of an ancient Anatolian petty king that she had visited with the benefit of a term's worth of university funds. As she made it to the summit after an arduous predawn climb, she saw in front of her a row of carved-stone deities, along with a representation of King Antiochus himself, set upon thrones of granite, all missing their heads due to an earthquake. In front of each body sat its complementary head, as if the statues were executed in a row as the result of some sort of transgression against the laws of nature, against the natural flow of life and death, in a mocking punishment of hubris. She especially remembered the face of a serpent god and that of a god in the form of a bird of prey. Fearsome, demonic looking gods, like Tio sitting in magmatic rage in front of her.

She, in turn, reckoned with the bloody crucifixes she had seen affixed in corners and above doors in Potosi and Sucre. They were terribly vivid, the face of Jesus always in agony. She was told by the tour guide at the Mint the previous day that they had been carved and painted in such a way by Indigenous artists, who felt that they understood the pain of Jesus first-hand because of their own mistreatment.

From here her home of Kentish Town in London felt foreign. And somehow wrong. An ocean and a continent away, it appeared as though she'd imagined it, an urban village of charm and taste, a den of artists and hipsters, where her doctor father and lawyer mother had renovated their turreted Victorian house, and where she spent many a night in her local pub and would head out to Leicester Square to the drinking establishments and clubs of central London. And where she, from time to time, had done cocaine, some of which no doubt came from this country. Could people in such faraway places ever imagine so many of the horrors here?

The others finished their kibitzing.

"Are you with us, Sally?" asked Rhonda. "We're on our way."

"Yeah, I'm with you," said Sally. As the group made their way back through the tunnel, the jerky movement of their lamps drawing a profile of their unsteady steps, she looked back at the shape of Tio as the statue was reclaimed by the dark, cloaked in the blackness as if forgotten back into the hidden unconscious of the mountain, like a dormant nightmare waiting once again to be brought to light.

Nothing so far. Not a single flinty bit of tin, not a modicum of silver. Nothing. It made Pablo wonder why on earth he did this day and day out, almost every day of the year. It made him wonder why he had ruined his lungs. He wiped the dripping sweat from his brow and leaned a moment on his pick, catching his wheezy, stertorous breath. Inside his lungs rattled and gurgled dirty phlegm. In a minute he would be ready to begin hacking at the walls again. The *chink chink chink* of Arturo's axe rang in the still air and circled the walls of the chamber before dying out, shaped and sent in a final dying echo up into the entrance tunnel through which they had shimmied into work hours before.

His wife had been giving him a look these past months, a loving, empathetic, sad look—a sweet smile that said, "You are not long for this world. Thank you for what you have done." He knew he was doomed, but he had thus far beaten the odds. Many didn't make it past ten years in the mines. Fewer still made it to fifteen. At twenty years in the mines, he was a grand old man, a grizzled minion of Tio himself, as he joked at the Friday afternoon celebrations often held in the presence of the statue itself. Pushing carts full of ore past the statue made him feel that he was indeed in some sort of earthly trial for hell. If hell was anything like commonly depicted, with subterranean slave labour under the scourges of scowling devils, then he was well-practised and had little to fear if that was where he was going when he wheezed his last.

Sweat was pouring off of him. He had long discarded his threadbare overshirt and was now in a T-shirt that used to be white but was now soaked with dirt and grime. It was hot down here. Surely in hell he would be hotter, his skin pinpricked by a million needles of heat, as though he were being unthreaded by the flames back into the carbon strands from which he was woven, but here it was hot enough. If they picked harder and deeper, they might just get there by dint of their own labours, picking and blasting to the source of heat, the lair of eternal punishment. Ha! Follow the path to "riches" all the way to hell!

Two weeks earlier, he had celebrated his birthday. With several other miners, he began drinking at the tunnel mouth, next to piles of slag and a row of parked slurry carts. The next he remembered he was at home shuddering ill in bed, his wife stroking his hair, looking at him with that sad smile, saying, "Did you have a happy birthday, Pablo?" Her own face was hard and worn, the face of someone who was both a mother and a smelter, picking through the broken heaps of ore trundled daily out of the catacombs in which no saints toiled in search of salvageable bits of metal. She did this for hours a day—in the heat, in the cold, in the rain, in the softly falling snow, in the bitter, knife-edged mountainside winds that tumbled over the slopes or roared from the other side of the valley, across the city, moaning through the flues of its alleys. She smiled and revealed with her smile her missing front tooth, the lines of her smile showing the love of someone with experience, someone with informed empathy. He loved her, and she loved him, they who had met on the cusp of adolescence, on the verge of budding so many years ago. Within three years they had their first baby, and he was by then several years in the mine, his lungs settling with dust like a pair of hourglasses running out of time.

As he wound up to swing his pick yet again, he heard behind him the voice of a man shouting, "*Hola! Turistas extranjeros!*"

"*Si, si,* okay!" hollered Pablo in return.

"*Bueno,*" Arturo said, smiling. "More coca! More gifts!" They heard the scratching and scraping sounds of people approaching through the tunnel. The first to emerge was a squat, heavy-set man with a wide, dark face and large, flat nose, clearly Bolivian like themselves. He lowered himself carefully into the chamber, calling out to those behind him, "Come, come, you're almost there!"

Pablo recognized him as Mario, a guide of some respectability, a man who had sensibly and luckily married himself out of the mountain life, though he returned time to time to lead tours or lend a hand.

Heralded by a small slide of gravel, a young woman emerged back first, her dangly, rubber-booted legs scratching for purchase as she lowered herself downward into the chamber, followed by a young man and another young woman. Each of them reached into their backpacks, from which emerged the familiar sight of plastic bags full of gifts—cigarettes, alcohol, coca, dynamite, bars of alkaline stone for dissolving coca and adding to its tingly effects.

"Hola," said the first woman in salutation as she adjusted her wobbly hard hat that had slid askew upon landing. The other woman and the young man did likewise, and Pablo nodded to them both, looking out of the corner of his eye as he hunched over, hands on knees, to catch his breath. He could hear Mario instructing them on the realities of the mine and the work of the miners. Then Mario approached and placed in front of him the bags of gifts.

Pablo turned and addressed them briefly, scarcely meeting their eyes. *"Gracias, amigos."*

Arturo did as well, thanking them before taking another swing at the tunnel wall. Pablo rummaged through one of the bags, finding a new pouch of coca leaves, and he spat out the macerated wad that had been lodged in his mouth for well over two hours now. He availed himself of the new ones and crumbled off with his fingertips a little soda stone from a fresh bar that, when mixed with the leaves and his saliva, would hasten its effect. Satisfied, he returned to work amid the chatter and observation of Mario and the tourists.

Mario called out to him, "Hey! One of the tourists wants to know how often you find silver."

Pablo smiled. "Every day." Mario related this to the three tourists, and his words were followed by nodding laughter in appreciation of Pablo's bleak wit.

"Another wants to know how old you both are and how long you have both been here in the mine."

Arturo answered, "Sixteen years old. Three years here."

"I am thirty-eight. Twenty years in the mine for me." As if to illustrate his length of time in the mine, he coughed on cue a white frost of dust that dispersed immediately in the darkness. Take a good look at me, he thought. Take a good look at me and show my picture to all your friends at home. Ha!

Just as he returned to his work, with the swing of his pick Arturo dislodged a large tablet of rock, which slid away like the cover of a burial crypt, revealing a modest vein of tin frozen in its flow, a mineral glacier cooled and set in its spidery network of canals reaching upward from the molten depths congealed in its tracks. Arturo and Pablo both grinned at this discovery, which was related to the others by Mario. Arturo, smiling, picked up a glittery stone from the shattered section of tunnel wall at his feet. It glinted in the half light thrown by the cones of the tourists' lamps. The discovery was commemorated by the flashing of cameras, the light scintillating off the facets of the cavern walls in flickering bursts.

Ah! Not so bad today, thought Pablo. This is something at least. I hope there is more. He allowed himself to smile at the tourists, who, it was clear from their gesturing and expostulating with Mario, wanted photographs of themselves with the miners. Why not, he agreed in his mind, why not? He stood next to the young man and grinned shyly but proudly with a closed mouth, hiding his metal fillings and his missing eyetooth, and Arturo, on the other the side, grinned widely. They posed with the two young women as well, both of them joining in at the same time, the camera clicking and bursting in a wash of light again in momentary clarity the cloven hefts of the cavern walls, the razorous angles of broken rock, the heaps of pulverized gravel, the weighted precipitate of millions of years.

Pablo and Arturo returned to their labours as the tourists and Mario stood by and observed, and they now used an air drill to prepare a blast of dynamite to free the tin from the rock. As it became apparent what they were preparing to do, Mario prudently ushered out the foreigners and himself shimmied up into the hole from whence they came, leaving the two miners to the duties of extracting blood from stone.

Through the ghostly depths of the mountain the tourists made their way like moles toward the light yet unseen beyond the bend in the tunnel in this underground labyrinth that refracted darkness off every twist and turn of its rocky corridors. It had been some time since they heard the blast, muffled and reduced to a thump akin to a foot pedal on a bass drum. Those two miners likely were now sifting their way through a pile of stones, coughing in an acrid murk of dust and hoisting their loot upward to awaiting carts, much like another handful of miners they had watched earlier, who'd winched by hand a bucket of ore that wobbled and swung like a wonky pendulum, bumping off the sides of a narrow shaft that faded into blackness. As Rhonda contemplated the sights and sounds she had thus witnessed, she was startled by a clanking trundle, the sound and vibration of weighted and metallic momentum.

"Los extranjeros! Cuidado! Los extranjeros! Cuidado!" A voice strained with effort and exertion. Rhonda and the others moved to the side as several miners pushed along a train of ore carts piled high with ore, bits of broken rock falling off and clattering to the floor of the tunnel as they charged ahead. Their faces streamed with sweat, and it poured off them in long, beaded dollops as they wrung themselves of moisture and energy in their exertion. She fumbled for her camera in the black camera bag, hurriedly snapping free the lens cap on its string and turning the camera on. It came to life with a brief whining adjustment of its telescopic lens like eyes fluttering open groggily after a long sleep. She managed three harried photographs as the muscle-powered train shunted by on iron wheels and piston legs, and as she replayed them using the camera's review

function, she noticed that of the three, two came out streaked and blurred. Oh, well.

"Did you get a good shot?" asked Mario as they continued on their way.

"Well, one of them turned out okay. It's pretty dark in here, so I have low expectations." Laughter. They forged onward, their breath smoking frost in the cool, moist air of the tunnel. Rhonda was reminded of the mountains of British Columbia, her home province, ascending into the sky and topped with snow as though it were rubbed onto the summits by the passing of the clouds overhead. And now she was in a high mountain, deep within its coiling bowels and the legacy of the men it had digested and was now digesting, and it was giving her the creeps. She did not like shimmying between levels on her hands and knees, the weight of the mountain mere inches over her head, a dense condensation of mass pressing downward under the spell of gravity. Nor did she like the fact that the various miners she saw digging and hoisting and hauling this morning were likely, to a man, to die as the result of their jobs, their lungs sputtering out on them after wearing away for years under a tyranny of settling silicate.

And yet. It was all so amazing. Nobody at home would believe this. Casually walking into a mine fraught with danger, moving freely about the worksites to which the locals were tethered with the invisible shackles of circumstance, of economic reality.

She felt her first pang of guilt when she was chastised for snapping a picture of the old lady in the alleyway when they were making their way to the tour agency. It was certainly a good picture, a great one even. Somewhat reminiscent of that famous National Geographic photo of the Afghan girl taken around 1979, the cowled young woman staring into the reader with her sea-green eyes and solemn yet resolute face—a portrait of strength and poignancy. A picture repeated and aged about thirty years this morning with a camera itself an updated version of the one that took that famous picture—an expensive Canon camera, no less, that she was just learning how to use. The trip throughout the mountains of the Altiplano had given her plenty of opportunity to learn the myriad features of this complex piece of equipment, this adjustable and telescopic electric eye that would see for her the world and capture likenesses of its permutations and approximate them in a digital matrix, an instant reduction of reality to painting by numbers. At roughly two thousand dollars it was hardly a steal, but Rhonda was eager to prove herself as an amateur photographer, trying to work her way into being a professional. To her parents' great chagrin, she had decided at the last minute to forego law school this year and had set about travelling throughout Colombia, Peru and Bolivia for several months to cut her teeth as a photographer, largely on money saved up working as an English teacher in Japan the two years previous. Her ex-boyfriend, Nigel, a fellow English teacher and himself from England, had worked for a small regional newspaper back in the U.K. before dropping everything for a life of international adventure, building a portfolio of travel photographs to try to sell to travel magazines. Inspired, she began teaching herself the techniques and held herself to her new hobby by buying an expensive camera. Now she had no choice but to take great pictures and to take them often. And here she was on her great South American odyssey doing just that. Her travels had taken her thus far up through the mountains of Chile into the Martian vistas of the Atacama Desert, through the shimmering dreamscape of the Salar de Uyuni, the world's largest salt desert and now into the heart of darkness itself—the diabolic dungeons of Cerro Rico. What a portfolio!

Beyond, a winking of light, the sun's semaphore. Away from the mountain's close and heavy embrace, these cloistered catacombs. Away from the ghosts—or were they just the wind? And away from the drip-dropping moisture like the tears of so many before wrung from the rocks into which they sweated and bled. Back to the city! Her belly growled for lunch, and soon she had to board a bus for Sucre, for what would surely be another clanking, shunting journey of discomfort slowed and stalled by mudslides or unforeseen mechanical problems on winding mountainside roads.

Outward ho! Approaching the light, its milky hue filtering into the dusty tunnel, the dust eddying this way and that, filling the vacuum that nature abhors, pulled by the shifting winds of passing bodies and outside breezes whispering in. Out, thank God! She squinted as the light filled her eyes in this heavenly arrival as she left this lithography of hell and walked into a wasteland of tumbled boulders, of tin shanties conglomerated from junk, a line of parked ore carts. A couple of miners stood near the tunnel's entrance, their faces as craggy as the slopes of the mountain, as though, through years of breathing in dust, they were made of the mountain themselves. They smiled and waved as they smoked and chatted.

The four tourists rubbed their eyes and adjusted their gaze. Below them sprawled the steeples and streets of Potosi. It was some distance to their awaiting van, as they had exited from a different tunnel from the one they had entered three hours ago. After a few minutes of crunching along the gravel path and enduring a dusty breeze that gritted against their teeth when they opened their mouths, with Rhonda snapping photos of the city, of the carts and of the shacks, Mario halted them for a demonstration of dynamite. He dug a small hole in the gravel with his hands and asked for a volunteer to do the honour of lighting a stick of dynamite, what looked to be a giant firecracker wrapped in white paper, a long fuse curling out of the top. Mario planted it in the hole as Jan volunteered, and Rhonda took a picture of Jan igniting the fuse, which sparked to life with a furious hiss. Mario and Jan dashed to a small gravel embankment and crouched with Sally and Rhonda. In this blasted wasteland, huddled to the gravel in their hard hats and waders, they resembled soldiers of the Great War bracing for a bombardment—which followed a moment later with a thumping concussion and a nearby shower of pebbles. As they stood giggling and remarking on the blast, they caught an acrid whiff of sulphur as the shreds of smoke from the explosion drifted their way on the wind. And on they went to the battered, dusty van awaiting them, where the driver, a-snooze in his seat, stirred into a sleepy semblance of duty and fumbled through his pockets for his keys at their noisy approach.

The door of the van slid open, and the tourists stepped in, the van tilting and groaning on its shocks as they bumbled about the interior and flopped onto the torn upholstery, the whitish-yellow foam spilling out from vinyl lacerations like fat from deep incisions. They cast off their hard hats and backpacks and broke into a noisy jocularity as the van began bouncing slowly as it wound down the mountainside road, the scenes of desolation scrolling by like a diorama, like an old fort with actors playing period soldiers in scarlet tunics with rapiers at their sides, and townsfolk and craftsmen going about their scripted errands—the butcher, the baker, the candlestick maker—all confined to playing their parts.

It wasn't a bad yield as yields go, and it seemed to go on, veins of tin splintering off into a lithic lacework of capillaries, leading them deeper into the mountain, closer to its molten heart. After a satisfying *almuerzo* above ground in the sun, Pablo and Arturo returned to the pile of stones left in the wake of their blast and hoisted bucket after bucket of ore two levels up to a train of hoppers. When the hoppers were full, they trundled the train out of the tunnel with their teeth clenched and sweat pouring from their bodies. Now they were putting the finishing touches on preparing for another blast, the bit of Pablo's air drill augering into the rock wall, the whining churring and grinding of metal through stone, the thudding vibrations rippling through his muscles and his bones, great drops of sweat swinging from grimy strings shaken and wrung from him. Finished, he put down the drill and turned to Arturo.

"I think it is time for a break." He wiped the sweat off his brow with his forearm.

"Good idea." Pablo moved away from the dust cloud he had created with his drilling and pulled out a cigarette, Arturo doing the same. The two smoked together in silence, tired but attuned to what they were doing, several hours into their shift and working like automata, their bodies acting according to the trained instinct of years on the job, their minds elsewhere, numbed, hypnotised by the repetitive and exerting chores to which they had subjected their bodies. They did not speak. By this point in the day, they did not need to, their tasks announcing themselves in sequence. Pablo had drilled a hole in the wall, and it was now time to pack that hole with dynamite and wire it to the fuse box and loose another lode of ore. Then they would once again hoist buckets of ore to a train of hoppers two levels up and once again haul the train clanking and trundling out of the tunnel. They worked in revolutions on a wheel bespoken for the demands of a distant market, a changeable abstraction beyond the summits of the Altiplano that announced itself in highs and lows of market fluctuations and sudden upsets like barometric pressure changes and the boom of thunder. They worked these revolutions ceaselessly under all weather and likely would not stop until death wrenched them free of this repetition like film snapping on a projector reel.

Arturo was in a daze, thinking now about nothing, really, as he inhaled the smoke, uninspired with the day save for the slight turn of fortune in the winds of the economy that had brought them, today, at least a modicum of tin. Random images filled his head—Christmas fireworks, a candy red Ferrari, Potosi at sunset. They called for attention and, spurned, faded away back into the recesses of his mind.

Pablo grunted something as he exhaled his smoke, though Arturo didn't for the life of him understand what he had said. Nor did he care.

"I said, what will you do tonight?"

"Nothing. Sleep, I guess."

A sardonic grin creased into being on Pablo's face. "Yes, sleep I would imagine. How is your head now?"

"Not bad. Better." He stubbed out his cigarette into the dust and squashed it underfoot. Pablo took one last drag on his cigarette, savouring the incense-like sweet scent of cloves, feeling in this pleasant burning a deep but subtle abrasion, a million tiny cuts from a spreading network of microfilaments slicing through the parched and fissured desert of his pulmonary tissues. Exhaling smoke and dust, he, too, stubbed out the remnants of his cigarette. As if responding to a telepathic command, Arturo stood and immediately rummaged through a plastic bag on the ground, the thin membrane of plastic crinkling as he did so, pulling from it a fresh stick of dynamite, a gift from the tourists. He then shoved it into the hole Pablo had just drilled, and into its twisted paper tip stuck the end of a wire attached to a cord which led its coiled and lazy way to a dusty, well-used fuse box.

"Good," approved Pablo. "Let's go." Pablo took the box in his arm, and Arturo fed the cable along, coil by coil. After Pablo disappeared into the tunnel, the cable now taut, Arturo followed him to safety.

"Ready?" asked Pablo, stooping over the box, hands clasped to the handle.

"Yes, ready," answered Arturo, squatting low and pressed to the wall, hands blocking his ears in anticipation. Pablo pushed down the handle. A moment later, there was a ricocheting concussion, followed by the waft of cordite, the smell of dust. They began crawling back to the tunnel, the smoke and dust washing acrid over them. Just as he was about to lower himself back into the chamber, Arturo was overcome by a thick sulphurous miasma, volcanic in intensity. He felt his muscles cramp and contort in painful spasms. His throat seized, and he felt himself shaking, lights dancing in front of his eyes. He tried to shout out to Pablo to warn him but couldn't push air through the closed vise of his throat. Then Pablo began gasping and choking behind him. As Arturo slithered and writhed in the dirt, hands on his throat, he turned and saw Pablo, his eyes bugged white, his face turning purple, his hands on his throat.

This is it, thought Arturo. This is it. I am going to die now in the mine. He thought of the gangsters at the movies, how he longed to step through the portal of the screen into a world of fantasy. He thought of his mother, his father, his brothers and his sisters. He thought of Tio looming over the mine, impassive, and how he was now tribute to this cruel god. All of these thoughts burst across his gaze at once as though disgorged from his convulsions. He saw above him in the beam of his jerking headlamp the contours of the tunnel, the scoring of stone, the grit of dirt, the lucent eddies of silicate and arsenic swirling in disruption. And to this ether of floating bodies was added the pinpoint lights of stars and nebulae shining in this anaerobic void, a whole universe stretching forth across his tortured gaze as foaming spittle gushed from his quivering lips and ran down his chin. He clutched with whitening hands at his own throat and soiled himself, his excrement sliding into his pants warm and wet and stinking. The universe stretched forth across his gaze, his world opening wide. And now would come the final eclipse, yes, the final eclipse as the darkness passed before him in a once-in-a-lifetime ultimate alignment of bodies with ominous astral certitude.

They lay contorted with their hands on their throats, the white dust settling mote by mote upon them in the blackness, their lamps still on, the beams crossed in the darkness as though blessing from above their forms in final absolution. Just beyond them in the chamber now filled with shattered rocks loosed by the blast, a broken vein of silver. A fee to pay the ferryman.

Jan was slightly dizzy. Alcohol hit him much quicker and harder at this altitude than it did at sea level, or below sea level back home. He sipped his Cusqueña beer, savouring the fizz as it needled his tongue, and he swallowed it with great satisfaction, basking in its inner glow.

He had been in South America for over two months now, working his way down through Chile, into Patagonia, and up through Argentina into Bolivia and then Peru. He had trekked through the magnificent spires of Torres Del Paine and the Fitzroy mountains in Patagonia, the stark and tapered pinnacles of rock spinning off clouds as though they were cotton. He had walked alongside frigid glacial lakes with forbidding Nordic names and through mossy glades of forest where fallen trees furred by moss and lichen lay in tumbled repose in the cool moist twilight under the forest canopy. And he had strolled through the sprawl of Buenos

Aires with its cathedrals, its galleries, then farther north through the wide and dusty avenues of colonial Salta, to the mighty tumbling cataracts of Iguazú Falls, spouting and cascading over the edges of the eroding shelves of the Iguazú River, waves of mist shimmering outward in iridescent waves as they caught the sun. And just yesterday, he had returned from a trek to Macchu Picchu, passing through its gates and wandering among the walls of great interlocking stones of various sizes, perfectly fit together, like a great construction of monumental puzzle pieces. There he saw the curtains of mist rise and expose the mountaintop shelf upon which Macchu Picchu roosted in its glory in a stone cohesion of Inca cosmology.

South America had for him thus far been a succession of sublimities, of experiences that he could never find, much less repeat back in Appledoorn, where he worked as a civil lawyer and where he had saved up for this trip of a lifetime he decided to take when he broke up with his girlfriend, Annelies. He had seized the opportunity of his newfound independence and had put off his melancholy for another day by setting off to forget himself awhile and fill the portholes of his perceptions with wonder.

Jan polished off his beer in a state of reverie. The café about him was abuzz, a foreigners' café doing brisk trade in providing familiar comfort food with a South American twist to the backpackers snaking their way along the Gringo Trail through South America. He had long finished his plate of *huevos rancheros* and was savouring his second beer. His stomach rumbled in protest, the combination of chili sauce with beans and beer potent and distending. An out-of-date *Vanity Fair* magazine, offered freely to patrons, sat splayed in front of him, the gloss of its open pages catching the light of the room, its edges curled up with age and the grease of a thousand perusing thumbs.

His knee ached. All the hiking these recent months had toughened him physically, but it had also accentuated certain areas prone to repetitive strain. Must I leave? he thought. I can scarcely walk. As he deliberated on whether to pay the bill and be gone, shuffling painfully through the alleys of Cuzco into the Plaza de Armas to sit and while away the hours on a park bench in the view of the Cuzco Cathedral or to flop in his tiny hotel room a mere three blocks away with its alley-brick window view.

A shape settled at the corner of his eyes as he glanced at the magazine. He looked up. Standing in front him was Rhonda from the mine tour in Potosi, smiling at him warmly.

"Rhonda," Jan said, startled. "Nice to see you! How are you?"

"Oh, good."

"Seen a lot this last while?"

"Quite a lot! You?"

"Oh, yeah."

"Hey, I need some lunch. Is the food good here?"

"The *huevos rancheros* are excellent."

A waitress approached, one of the owners, a middle-aged expatriate Englishwoman with highlighted blonde hair, a tawny figure. She had a narrow face lined from hard experience, and a humorous twinkle with a hint of brusqueness in her eyes.

"Can I take your order?" she intoned nasally in an English Midlands accent. "Busy at the moment, innit?"

"Certainly is," answered Rhonda. "I'll have the *huevos rancheros* and a cappuccino please."

"Good choice," said the waitress as she scribbled the order on her little notepad then looked at Jan. "And anything else for you?"

"I will have a *café con leche*, please."

"Righto, will do. Back in a mo'," she said with a grin and disappeared into the noisy bustle about.

"So, where've you been these last weeks?" asked Rhonda.

"Oh, here and there. After Potosi, I went to Uyuni and checked out that graveyard for old trains in the desert. Spooky. Like the aftermath of a nuclear war."

"Ah, the *Cementerio de Trenes*."

"Then, across the salt flats in a jeep."

"Aren't those amazing?"

"Yes. Incredible. Like another planet or something. What did you do after we parted ways?"

"Well, I left right after and went to Sucre."

"Potosi was such an interesting place. All those crucifixes and empty streets. You can tell bad things have happened there."

"The mine was a real trip."

"Crazy we went there. I think about it often."

"Actually I went back to Potosi a few days later so I could get a few more shots of the place."

"Really?"

"Would you like to see them?"

"Sure."

Rummaging through her backpack, Rhonda pulled out a small carrying case for a laptop computer. She brought it to life just as the English waitress returned with their beverages. "I've put together quite an album this last while." She loaded up the picture files in her computer and turned the computer so that they could both share in the experience. She clicked on a folder entitled "Potosi" and selected the option to display the pictures as a slide show. One after another the pictures faded in and faded out, bringing into pixel clarity the alleys of Potosi, the palsied, trembling Quechua woman, a streaked and smudgy view from the window of the van showing a ramshackle hut. A shot of the group of them standing at the tunnel's mouth, and another showing the scowling face of Tio as the group downed drinks around him. A picture of two miners hoisting up a bucket with an automatic winch and another with men pushing an ore cart. And a portrait of the two miners they had met who had struck tin in their section of the mine, the older one with a haggard, creased and papery face, the other one callow and chubby and youthful. On and on the pictures went, with Jan commenting on them every so often.

"Now, this is after you guys left," Rhonda said. "As I was walking through the streets, there was this funeral." A series of photos of a long Latin funeral procession appeared. One by one the pictures faded in and out in silence. There were throngs of mourners, many of them sobbing. Two brown caskets bedecked with flowers were carried on the shoulders of squat men with deeply scored faces, stoic and sombre and tough in their resolve. Altar boys carried a tall cross like a standard into battle in some medieval religious crusade. Close-ups showed charms and talismans and other tokens of Indigenous faith syncretised into Catholicism. One poignant close-up showed a sobbing older woman in a long red dress, poncho, and bowler cap, flabby, teeth missing, with a wrinkled face and her hand up on one of the coffins, tears streaming from her pained eyes. Her sad children around her, their faces down. Finally, there was a wide-angle shot of mourners entering the cathedral.

"These are some very good pictures," Jan mused as he sipped his coffee. "Will you post these on a website or something like that?"

"Yep, that's the plan. I'm trying to cut my teeth as a photographer." She smiled a little sheepishly. "I know, we all want to do something different. Be something unique."

Another day, and a new microbus of tourist disembarks at the mouth of a tunnel entrance, the area littered with decay. The four tourists, this time from America, America, Australia and Germany, respectively, duck behind a revetment of gravel and detritus as

Mario blasts a stick of dynamite for their amusement, and then the five of them together enter the tunnel, walking along the rails into the awaiting blackness.

Today is a busy day in the mine. They can hear in the distance shouting voices, the weighted trundle of carts, the screech of metal wheels on metal rails. As they walk ahead, a team of men shout for them to get out of the way. With little advanced warning, a train of carts bears down, pushed by eight sweaty, straining, grunting men. Not long after another man-powered ore train shunts by on heaving flesh-and-bone pistons. Miners pass them, walking in and walking out on their various rotations of duties. Amid the bustle they make their way to the chamber of Tio, presiding over the dungeon depths of his domain.

As they observe, their senses heighten, their ears making up for what their eyes cannot see save for faint outlines and the glittering trickle of water flashing like flecks of mica in the sweeps of their lamplight. Mario thinks to himself of the tragedy of all the days experienced in the mine by all the men who worked its seams. He thinks of it graphically, he, being an untrained and frustrated artist sent to the mines to toil and ruin his hands. He pictures Albrecht Dürer’s portrait of praying hands modelled after those of Dürer's brother who toiled so that the great artist could study. Mario had seen a reprint of this work once in an ESL workbook in a class he attended in Melbourne in Australia, where he’d moved with his wife Suzanne and where he now teaches Spanish, his second language after Quechua, his only exportable skill.

Mario recalls this image every time he comes back to the mine where his hands had been hardened into creased and calloused leather gloves, mashed, cut, crushed, burned, banged, numb and tremulous with the vibrations of the drills, shaped by the crude forces unleashed in the smithy of experience.

The tourists stand in the chamber, oohing and aahing appropriately to the statue of Tio wreathed in his usual garb of desiccated offerings, a cigarette still jutting from his mouth. Around him and above his head set into niches in the wall are many totems, little statues of Tio with scary scowling faces like tiny impish minions of the underworld.

“Man, he looks evil,” says one of the tourists, a young and hyperexcitable American man.

“Underground is Tio’s kingdom,” Mario explains as he had countless times before. He sees in a flash in his mind’s eye the human tribute parading through the streets, the crying women, the coffins borne high aloft on the shoulders of the compatriots of the dead. Another scene unpainted by his ruined hands.

Tio looks down upon him in his fixed scowl.

Camera flashes and poses, a drink offering to Tio, alcohol poured on shoulders, knees, penis, feet. Mario waves them on with ruined hands now partly numb.

In their absence Tio dissolves into blackness, into the unconscious of the mine, brooding and awaiting tribute, a nightmare to be had again in time.

For in the tunnels of the mountain, Tio reigns supreme.

GREY

FOUND DIVINATION

Ursula Pflug

Every day I'd walk to Burrard Inlet to watch the ships pass under mountains or to Commercial Drive to meet an old friend or scribble in a coffeehouse. I'd marvel at the little libraries, seemingly one on every other street. A few years ago, I found Butler's *Parable of the Sower* in a little library in Hanalei, not far from the beach. I didn't read it in Kaua'i but put it in my already overstuffed carry-on for when I got home. It was just as good as I'd heard, maybe better, brimming with a prescience almost eerie in the ways the story held to our world now.

So much so that I read looking for clues:

What do we do now? Where do we go? How do we get there?

Ever since then I've checked little libraries. There may be something better than pet care, out-of-date travel guides, or Jodi Picoult and James Patterson novels, all power to them, sort of.

In a little library I found on my way to the Drive, there was a book with a homemade paper cover, plain white. I took it out and opened it to see if the original cover was damaged, but it wasn't. Someone had made the new cover for another reason, maybe to demonstrate to a child how it was done, especially the wonderfully tight-fitting folded corners.

For my own kids I didn't make folded-paper book covers but origami birds and frogs and balloons, putting them on the Christmas tree. I showed my children and their friends and the children at their schools how to make them in those years before they all grew up and left for school and travelling. I followed them to become a wanderer again. I went to Neuruppin and Miyajima and Barra de Navidad, Atenas and Poli Hale, to find humans or Lemurians or Arcturians of whom I might ask:

What do we do now? Where do we go? How do we get there?

Inside the white homemade cover was a book about the night sky, the one we had before the arrival of the permanent haze. We have lost the stars and don't know them anymore. Even if we want to learn them, we can't see enough of them to do so. In Hawai'i when I look up, I see Scorpio instead of the familiar dippers and Orion of my Ontario childhood. Cassiopeia appears in both the northern and tropical skies, but in a different location, and maybe the bears and the hunter's belt are also there, just tucked away in unfamiliar corners and at unexpected angles.

I am going back soon, and I look forward to seeing Scorpio overhead. The Scorpion's red heart is the star Antares. On Kaua'i, Reddit people talk about Lemuria, of which Hawai'i is allegedly a part. Another red star, Arcturus, is also much discussed, largely because Arcturians are known to be helpful. And we all know we need help. I once saw Arcturians on Kaua'i when I was young, but it was after I'd ingested a copious amount of *Panaeolus cyanescens* mushrooms, a powerful tropical species we used to gather in the old pastures on the shoulders of the Sleeping Giant near Anahola. No, don't go. And even if you wanted to, the old cane-haul roads we used to take to get there were all closed long ago.

Unfortunately, I forgot to ask the Arcturians: What do we do now? Where do we go? How do we get there?

Forgot to ask the mushrooms or the aliens? Perhaps the Arcturians were also ingesting copious quantities of Copelandia, another name for Paneoulus. It was so long ago that, had I received an answer from shrooms, aliens, or aliens on shrooms, it might no longer be relevant.

We need a new answer for a new time.

As I had the Butler, I thought I might read the dark-sky book from the East Van little library at home, if I could fit it in my overstuffed carry-on. When I leafed through it, two beautiful cards fell to the sidewalk. I read tarot for years when I was young. I still have notebooks full of scribbled readings to prove it, as I found out reading my way through cartons of them the first pandemic winter and later when the heat waves and smoke from the continental forest fires forced us inside. I didn't scan the meanings of my old readings. There were too many and, like my meeting with the Arcturians, it was too long ago. What would the Arcturians think of this world we're destroying with our endless greed?

We need answers for now. Answers to save Mother Earth, to save ourselves.

The cards were both from what I assumed was an oracle deck, titled "Open Centre" and "Natural Abundance." Maybe not tarot, though folks are constantly designing new decks in which they rewrite the names of the suits and the Major Arcana. It can be hard to tell when you've only got a couple of cards to make your guess.

Right away, I wondered what the cards signified. I could pretend they were my reading for the day, or maybe for my Vancouver trip. I could put the two-card found divination in a story, so you, too, could feel a bit of the wonder I felt, walking every day those streets of blue and purple wooden houses so beautiful they seemed not quite real. And on each street a little library full of marvels.

What adds to the mystery is that I'd just purchased a book of stories for my e-reader, to read at night while I scribbled during the day. I filled yellow legal pads and spiral-bound Hilroy notebooks at Konrad's little desk in the window, where mountains greeted me early each morning, slowly emerging as the stars, such as they were, said good night.

In *The New Wave Fabulists*, edited by Peter Straub, a magician we lost not long ago, there are stories by Kelly Link and Neil Gaiman, China Miéville and Elizabeth Hand. In the story by Liz Hand, the protagonist goes to a jumble sale in the small town in Maine where she lives and buys a silk-wrapped packet of cards. The cards are blank, the backs printed in a design of spoked wheels in fading primary hues.

Except for two:

> But very slowly, I felt the cards separate. Maybe the warmth of my touch helped, or the sudden exposure to air and moisture. For whatever reason, the cards suddenly slid apart so that I held one in each hand. "Oh." I cried aloud; they were that wonderful. Two tiny, brilliantly inked tableaux like medieval tapestries, or paintings by Brueghel glimpsed through a rosace window . . . .

Hand's plot, which is also about tattoos and families, found divination and otherwheres, turns on the two mysterious oracle cards. I'd hoped, a little, the plot of my life, if not this story I'm working on, would be illuminated by the cards I'd found by equally mysterious circumstances. I'd come upon the cards during the day and chosen her story to read that evening. The two events made an impression on me, finding the cards and reading the story, one after another on the same day. They amplified one another.

From Google images I learned about the oracle cards' designer, Lili Acuña. She writes: "Each Spiral Oracle card is a mirror of your own inner world with the potential to reveal valuable information that lives within you." This is a trenchant way to describe what happens with any system of divination deployed in the right frame of mind. In another story I write about the *I-Ching* and about designing our own oracles, including the requisite spirit in which that project must be undertaken.

I think maybe it's not the found cards that had meaning, but the synchronicity. And if they did have meaning, it's opaque to me. The meanings, or inspirational messages as Acuña calls them, aren't posted on her website, and I'm not about to spend US$ 50.00 to purchase the deck, not even to find out the meanings of two cards that appeared in my life as if by magic.

Not doing it gives this story a different ending than if I had. For what if they'd provided insight into my questions: What do we do now? Where do we go? How do we get there?

Maybe I could write the deck off as a research expense. I did write to Lili, or whoever manages her correspondence, via the contact form. I told her how I acquired the two cards, though I left out the Liz Hand coincidence. Finding the cards is intriguing enough by itself, and I thought Lili might like the story enough to write me back.

Nothing yet.

The paintings "Natural Abundance" and "Open Centre" are located beside each other in the deck. There is another one, the only line drawing, depicting a woman looking at mountains, drinking tea. The caption reads: "*Oteando las montañas, tomando un mate*" and even though it describes my life house-sitting for Konrad in Vancouver, in this case, seeing a pattern seems ambitious.

I've never forgotten how some say you should make up your own meanings, that the first meaning you make will be the right one, just as some say the first page you write will be the right one. This is mine.

HOTHOUSE LOVE

Michael Mirolla

Gentle Mother, Dear Sisters and Brothers,
May you continue to grow straight and tall, may your limbs remain supple, may the sweet Earth nourish and keep you healthy all the days of your lives. Above all, may you mercifully escape the fate awaiting our more unfortunate brethren in the years, centuries and eons to come—and, no matter what happens, may you have the strength and wisdom to go on giving thanks.

Since it's my turn for storytelling and, since no one's permitted to shirk this duty—especially now that the Sleepers are on the verge of returning (hovering at this very moment like giant, black-winged angels in our pristine skies), I'd like to relate a tale from the dawn of time itself, one that I feel is more appropriate—and urgent—than ever. Yes, I'd like to tell the story of how Bob the Preacher and his good friend the No-Name Puppy saved a dying Earth from total and utter annihilation.

To begin with, his name wasn't Bob the Preacher in those days. Rather, if he called himself anything, it would have been Robert the Hobo. The "Hobo" in keeping with his lowly station in life: neither well-nourished nor well-rooted. And "Robert" because he truly disliked his childhood name of "Bob." It reminded him of bobbing for apples when such things were still in vogue. And "Bob's your uncle." And bob style haircuts. If someone had called him Bob before his preaching days, he would most likely not have responded —or responded in such a way as to let the person forcibly know how he felt about the name.

Needless to say, being a hobo with no place in which to retreat or take shelter, the winters proved to be extremely hard for Robert. Especially as he'd chosen one of the northernmost island-cities as his home during a period when climate control wasn't what it is today. Many a time, he would roam along this city's icy shoreline (jogging and bicycle paths in more clement weather), a thin layer of fibreglass insulation stuffed in his coat the only protection from the wind that came off the water with all the ferocity of a timber wolf. Timber wolf: *Canis lupus occidentalis* with glowing red eyes, drooling jaws and a tendency to howl. Once extinct, only recently re-constructed and, perhaps, soon to be extinct again.

But, if the days were untenable, you can just imagine the nights. Or maybe you can't in the midst of your typically tropical Eden, spoiled sisters and brothers. When that hazy orange ball sank below the horizon, glittery on the iced fountain-sprays of water, the entire landscape would take on the appearance of a Plutonian moon—blistered and lethal for even the smallest patch of exposed flesh. And each night Robert prepared without wasted motion for the end, for that moment the sap inside him ran dry for the last time. He would slide down quietly against the nearest leeward wall and—head between his knees—fall into a deep sleep, half-expecting not to wake up in the morning. And then he could imagine himself staying in that position, like a slender weeping willow—or birch tree—

broken-backed with snow, until the spring thaw brought warmth and renewed hope for the living and simple putrefaction for him.

It would have happened that way, too—if it hadn't been for "the miracle." Or rather the first in what is now a well-thumbed catalogue. Robert was crouched low against the side of a strange-looking structure that multiplied and reflected the setting sun in all its ghastliness and fare-thee-well splendour when he suddenly fell through one of the wall panels. Inside, it was palely dark, palely luminescent, with faint lights, it seemed, immense distances off. A blast of suffocatingly humid air took his breath away for a moment. He began to sweat beneath his layers of insulation. Salty drops obscured his vision, and everything around him turned green and shimmery, as if he were seeing the world through a steamy shower curtain. But he didn't care if he were swimming in his own sweat, if every single cell in his body began to itch intolerably from the heat, if he were in danger of literally melting. He knew one thing and one thing only—he was warm, and the warmth was delicious. For the first time in weeks, he stuck his head out from where it had been jammed inside his collar to conserve heat. And he untwined his fingers. And he wiggled his toes.

"Replace the wall panel," a deep voice told him. "Or else the winter will follow you in like a highly unwelcomed guest."

Of course, that was Robert talking to himself, something he had been doing with great frequency in recent weeks, as few of the people he met seemed interested in starting up a conversation—even after an act of kindness such as dropping a monetary unit of some kind into his outstretched palm. Not that Robert really minded, having always preferred his own company to that of others. Besides, what his own voice told him was normally good advice. So, he pushed the panel back into its slot. Several of the screws were loose —a stroke of luck that explained why it had fallen in the first place.

He re-tightened them enough for the panel to hold—but not so he couldn't make a quick getaway the moment someone unexpectedly rattled the front door. For he knew that, even in the wintertime, maintenance was needed to keep such a place going.

He wiped the perspiration from his eyes and, as he became accustomed to the dark, had his first good look around. There were plants everywhere—ferns and trees and vines of all kinds. He could hear fans high on the roof, blowing down hot air. Most of the plants had little lighted name plates in front of them. A very few didn't. He realized then he was in a greenhouse—and that explained the reflection of the sun earlier in the evening. The higher portions of the building were made of large glass plates to capture as much daytime heat as possible. Why, look, from here Robert could even see the moon and a few of the stars—a miracle in itself in those days of perpetual smog.

Robert decided then and there to make the most of it. He didn't expect to stay in the greenhouse more than one night, as the loose panel would definitely be spotted and fixed by the first worker to come in. But one night was one more than he'd counted on. Like a reprieve, a temporary commutation of the sentence. So, he took off his coat, the one stuffed with fibreglass insulation, and wrapped it into a serviceable pillow —along with his greasy tuque and oversized mittens (the ones legend has it had been knitted by his invalid mother so many years before). Then, he removed his steel-toed boots and placed them to one side where he could reach them quickly—for fleeing or defence. Finally, he lay on his back and, taking the liberty of stretching (something he hadn't done since the temperature had dipped below zero), cartilage and ligaments snapping from disuse, he stared at the dark mass of leaves above him, their undulating and slightly glowing shadows lulling him gently but firmly to sleep.

It was, however, a strange kind of sleep—and filled with dreams that came in rapid succession, almost superimposed on one another. Of those he remembered the next morning, Robert couldn't quite decide if they were idyllic or nightmarish, full of hope or weighed down with foreboding. He dreamt at one point of a jungle, which he found only natural in a greenhouse setting. But this was a jungle like no other. It was filled with underground tunnels where the roots of 300-metre-tall trees were being severed one by one, gnawed by giant rodents with electric hedge-clippers instead of teeth. And he dreamt of a city. Or a place that had once been a city and that might someday be a city again. At the moment, it seemed to be between phases, like one of those pictures that changes shape depending on which way you tilt it. And finally, he dreamt of jungle and city together, speeding towards some sort of dénouement that was beyond him, that gave him a headache just thinking about it.

In the morning, Robert awoke with a start—as if someone or something had brushed his face gently to warn him. And a warning was exactly what it had been. He scrambled out of the greenhouse, a few steps ahead of the city employee whose job it was to make sure the temperature controls functioned properly. Perhaps there was no need for such haste, Robert thought, once he was outside and looking across a frozen river from which the mist rose like dirty dry ice. Perhaps the employee might have greeted him with a pleasant, "Hello, friend." And, "Would you like to share a cup of Java?"

Perhaps. But Robert couldn't take the chance. The last public service employee he'd encountered had kicked him squarely in the chest as he lay on a heating grill just inside one of the city's subway stations. The insulation was the only thing that saved him from broken ribs and slow death from internal bleeding. So, without a second thought, he had bid his steamy paradise farewell and hurled himself into the cold, barely managing to pull the panel up behind him.

"That's the end of that," he told himself, feeling the sharp cold bite at his lungs. "But who cares, eh?"

> Among so many people cozy in their home
> I am like a man who explores far-off oceans.
> Days with full stomachs stand on their tables;
> I see a distant land full of images.

Now, where the hell did I get that tidbit from? Ah, of course. "The Solitary Person." Rainer Maria Rilke. One of my very favourites."

The words, coming to him on their own, uninvited, were like glimpses of another time. For Robert the Hobo had once been Robert the High School English Teacher—when such things still existed or mattered. And his head was full of similar nonsense, snatches of verses for every occasion. Or none. But this time he was wrong. It wasn't the end of anything. When he returned that night, after a day spent at the bottom of a subway-station escalator, hand thrust out and hoping against hope, he fell through the same panel into the same greenhouse.

"They missed it! Goddammit, they missed it! I don't know how —and I don't care—but they did."

And he rubbed his hands with glee as he replaced the panel for the second time. It was only after he'd removed his coat and prepared to settle down for another miraculous night that he noticed a small form by his feet. At first, it seemed inert. But then it began to shudder, as if it couldn't control its own movements. Boot in hand, ready to strike in case of attack, Robert leaned over to get a better look. And then quickly lowered his boot.

"Sweet Jesus. How did you get here?"

It was a puppy. Soon to be *his* puppy, his No-Name Puppy. A ragged mop with floppy ears and enormous eyes that practically glowed in the dark. But there's no need to describe it in detail, is there? Anyone who wishes may still see it (if they hurry, that is), immortalized for future generations in the nearby park. At the time, it was still unaware of its destiny, still unsure of what would come next. So, the tiny creature cowered as Robert brought his hand down to pet it. Then, realizing the man meant no harm, it reached up to lick his fingers.

Robert and the puppy slept side by side that night, the puppy snuggled against the man's chest, trying to get at his nipple. There were more dreams for Robert. They made, if possible, less sense than the ones from the previous night. And it seemed, the several times Robert awoke after a particularly vivid one, that even the puppy whimpered convulsively.

In the morning, Robert was startled awake by the sound of an unearthly yelp. What he saw had him rubbing his eyes in disbelief. There, suspended above him and being slowly pulled up into the sky, was the puppy. It struggled and cried in the grasp of one of the vines, releasing a stream of urine and defecating mightily. But nothing helped. Up the poor, frightened, shit-encrusted creature went, up towards the maw of a darkly foliated plant that had no nameplate. Robert envisioned the bones being spit out one at a time. Or perhaps dissolved in corrosive acid that effectively reversed the roles of predator and prey.

"No!" Robert the Hobo screamed and at the same time realized the futility of his gesture. How could screaming at a plant, albeit a carnivorous one, produce results?

But it seemed to. The vine hesitated, quivering, rocking back and forth. It held the puppy just beyond reach for a moment, as if weighing it. Then gently let it down. The second the puppy hit solid ground, it scrambled to hide behind Robert's leg and let off several volleys of barking before another feint from the vine made it go mute. The vine hovered above Robert's head, weaving about like a snake.

Robert could sense, however, that this was no "ordinary" carnivorous plant and that it meant him no harm. Or rather, that the word "harm" didn't exist in its vocabulary. It reached down and, before he had a chance to react, stuck a sucker to his temple. Immediately, he had the same visions as the two nights gone by. Only now he knew they weren't dreams, at least not the kind met in sleep. And the images, crystal-clear and sharply focused, made complete sense to him. Though he fervently wished some of them might not.

"You're the human we've been looking for," came the voice inside his head, mercifully clearing away the images before they became unbearable—like trapped sheets of lightning, flashing back and forth, ever-increasing in amplitude till . . . till the necessary explosion, the smell of burnt bark. Or sizzling, totally fried neurons.

Amid the puzzlement, the frazzled scramble to understand, Robert knew one thing. This was definitely not his own voice this time, not that internal orator reciting fragments of favourite rhymes or carrying on imaginary conversations with people who didn't even speak his language. For one thing, it was a soft voice, described as feminine when such differences were still being observed.

"What do you want with me?" he said, a split-second before his mouth actually formed the question. Telepathy. That was it. He had heard of that.

"You know that already, don't you? What is the meaning of those words we find in your head:

> The tulips are too excitable, it is winter here.
> Look how white everything is, how quiet, how snowed-in.
> I am learning peacefulness, lying by myself quietly
> As the light lies on these white walls, this bed, these hands.

"'I am nobody; I have nothing to do with explosions,'" Robert said, continuing the verses. "It's from a poem. Something called "Tulips" by an ancient poet named Sylvia Plath."

"Yes, we know that," the vines said, waving as if impatiently. "But what do they mean? What's their significance?"

"Significance?" Robert creased his brow. "You wouldn't understand. It's a poem from a time of intense neurosis. You have to be human to understand it. Besides, there aren't poems or neuroses anymore, so there's no chance of understanding now, even if you were human."

"Ah, we see now."

> And I have no face, I have wanted to efface myself.
> The vivid tulips eat my oxygen.

"Death. They have to do with death. Death we understand very well. A yanking, is it not? An unimaginable snipping away? A loss of contact with the good earth itself? The ultimate unrooting? Precisely what is happening at this very moment."

They did understand. Robert the Hobo suddenly felt very tired, as if he were being drained of some essential fluid. Or pulled down by gravity. His arms fell by his sides. His legs were rubber beneath him. He didn't know how he was still standing, what was holding him up.

"We are sorry," the voices said, obviously reading his thoughts. "We didn't realize how quickly your species tires. Must be all the effort you put into individuation. And external armour. Very impressive armour, we must add."

The vine just as suddenly released him. He fell head-first to the ground, his face in the warm loam. From where he was lying, he saw another tentacle make its way towards the wall panel. Robert knew now he had gone crazy, had definitely gone over the edge. For wasn't that the vine carrying a screwdriver, one of those with interchangeable heads? And not only carrying it but seeming to know what to do with it, which one to use. Yes, the men in the white coats would come soon and take him away. The hospital was quite close. At least it would be warm in there, and the porridge, he'd heard, was excellent. If he made enough of a fuss, they might even put him in an isolation ward. That would be exquisite. No one to talk to but himself. The vine pressed the screwdriver against the panel and removed the screws. Then it pulled the panel away from the wall. The cold air revived Robert somewhat.

"You must leave now, as the workers are coming. But make sure to return this evening. We'll send the puppy with you as a reminder. Goodbye."

Robert the Hobo stumbled out, hopping about in the snow as he dressed and slipped his boots on one at a time. The panel was immediately replaced behind him—and just as quickly screwed back in. Robert remained standing in the same spot for several minutes. Inside, he could see the day's first worker going about his job. The man, wearing dirty brown overalls, was whistling. He checked the thermostat right beneath the plant that had just recently communicated with Robert, had asked him about poetry and death, no less. Robert didn't know very much about plants, but this one looked quite ordinary to him: a thick central stalk several metres high from which issued, at various levels, tentacles of leafy vines. Nothing unusual or frightening about it—no sticky maw, no thought projection, no display of manual dexterity.. Everything seemed normal, except, perhaps, for the fact it had no name plate.

Robert spent the day, or as much as there was of it, in the public library researching carnivorous plants. He was thankful the facility had been abandoned and sealed up long before, as no one actually borrowed or read manuscripts any longer. He recalled vividly the days spent in crowded public libraries, hundreds of humans on all sides—beside him, above and below him—and how uncomfortable he had found it to be among so many people in such an enclosed space.

He shuddered. The memory brought back all the reasons why he had taken to the road in the first place—the claustrophobia, the xenophobia, the misanthropy that had plagued him even when he was in the classroom teaching, standing in front of thirty boisterous, hyperactive and ultimately uncaring teenagers who wanted nothing more than to slip a whoopee cushion under his seat. And he remembered very well the day he finally broke down, viciously attacking a pretty high school senior in a cashmere sweater who'd innocently asked him why they didn't study Leonard Cohen (a poetaster of the late 20th century who became popular after he abandoned poetry for song jingles). That had been followed by psychiatric tests, discovery of deep unresolved emotional problems, threats from irate parents and finally a resignation one step ahead of outright dismissal.

But there was no one else in this public library, except for his puppy, of course, busy marking his territory. The walls of the monumental building were being forced apart by the ebb and flow of ice, the successive thawings and freezings. The ceiling leaked brown water where the pipes had burst. One more winter and the huge marble blocks of its central stairway would come tumbling down in a heap. Inside, the books, those that hadn't been chewed by rats or scavenged for rolling papers, now flowered with icy mould.

Room after room in democratic disarray. Aristotle coupled with Jacqueline Susann. *Cybernetics* rubbing spines with *The Classless Society*. Bibles and Korans too close for comfort. Still, after several hours of searching through the rubble, Robert was able to find what he was looking for: a book on the carnivores of the plant world. But it didn't help him much. The largest carnivorous plant yet discovered was something called the *Sarracenia flava 'Maxima'* or Trumpet Pitcher, which rose to a height of three feet. The biggest things it could capture were bluebottle flies and wasps, which had once made it popular with housewives concerned about damage to the environment from insect repellents.

Besides, it had no tentacles or vines to hold its prey. Instead, it relied on luring the insects down its throat with nectar till they were in too deep to escape. Like marriage, Robert thought, smiling. Or, come to think of it, like any relationship with another human being. This was definitely not the plant at the greenhouse. In fact, search as he might through the volumes on botany, he could find nothing resembling that plant. Maybe it wasn't so ordinary after all.

"A hybrid, of course!" Robert exclaimed. "These mad scientists are always creating hybrids these days. New ones all the time. A secret experiment being conducted by the government—and I've stumbled on to it. They're teaching plant life how to communicate with humans and how to use screwdrivers. In preparation for advanced jungle warfare. No more defoliation. All you do is make the plants your allies and let them attack the enemy for you. Isn't that so, puppy?"

The puppy let off chewing and wagged its tail.

"If that were so," a quiet voice inside Robert said, "then why did the plant let you in on the secret? And where's the security that would normally surround such a project? They'd be using atomic minefields to keep people away."

Robert couldn't shake the distinct feeling the voice was coming from the puppy.

"Naah, it can't be," he said, shaking his head while staring into the puppy's opaque eyes. "Not telepathic dogs, too!"

"You're right. I'm not a telepathic dog. I'm part of the same organism you left behind at the greenhouse. And it's about time you headed home to us, don't you think? There's lots of work to do before you're ready—and time presses."

"Before I'm ready for what?"

"Before you're ready to save the world, of course."

"Save the world?" Robert said, his laughter echoing in the huge room. "What, are you nuts or something?"

"Nuts? No, we believe nuts belong to an entirely different family of plants altogether."

"Well, good for them," Robert said, standing up and turning away in the hope of breaking contact. "But you're not getting me anywhere near that place again. No sir. I'd rather take my chances in the middle of a gender-identity lawyers' convention. Or riding the subway at rush hour with a bunch of Jesus freak muckers."

"You were given a choice," the voice said as the puppy followed at his heels. "And the opportunity to back out. But you've already made your decision. It's too late to go back on it now. We're very sorry."

"Oh, it's too late, is it?" Robert said, hoping the sarcasm was dripping through from his head to theirs. "Just watch me, and then we'll see who's sorry."

But watching Robert at that moment would have been a very painful experience. He collapsed suddenly to the marble-veined floor, clutching his head. Rather, clawing at it would be a more apt description, as if trying to pull something out of it. Then he began to writhe in a circle, using his head as a pivot and all the while screaming "No!" over and over again till the library was filled with his voice, echoed back and forth with his howls. Finally, he lay there moaning, his tongue darting convulsively in and out of his mouth.

Robert never told anyone what he saw or felt or experienced during those few excruciating seconds. Some say it was a vision of the end of the world so ghastly it turned his eyeballs inside out. Others proclaim it a sight of such exquisite spiritual beauty it broke his heart and vaporized his soul. Whatever it was, Robert arose from his trance a different man. And he followed quietly, zombie-like, as the puppy pranced and capered his way back to the greenhouse in the middle of the winter's worst snowstorm.

Once inside again, Robert sat down cross-legged directly in front of the plant—and didn't even flinch when the tentacle slithered through the air and attached itself with a "suck-a-suck" to the side of his head.

"Hello, Bob," the voice said, the epitome of gentleness. "You don't mind if I call you Bob, do you?" Bob shook his head. "Good. Bob's a nice name, isn't it? You can even say it backwards without anyone noticing the difference. Unlike 'god' or 'metonymy.' You're probably saying to yourself right about now, 'What the hell do they want with me?' That is what you're thinking, no?" Bob nodded. "Well, as a matter of fact, we do want you for something, something of extreme importance, something that is only possible at this particular time and at no other. You see, Bob, we need you to help save the Earth. Your days as an outcast and renegade are definitely numbered. Soon, you'll be by far the most important member of the entire human race, with responsibilities that would crush you if you had to bear them alone. Fortunately, we're here to lend support. We've been empowered, mandated, to bring it about. And we can't afford to miss the opportunity, for our time is limited, and it might never come again. Together, we'll try to undo the harm that's been perpetrated. We'll labour to repair the wounds. We'll seal up the pus-infested sores. We'll restore the Earth to its pristine beauty. Forever and ever. Let us show you how."

Bob, no longer a hobo but not quite a preacher either, toppled over on his side and slept. He slept throughout the rest of the winter. Not once did he move, not even to twitch an eyebrow or shake a leg. In fact, a sort of greenish cocoon grew around him where he lay. By some chemistry unknown to human science, the puppy performed all Bob's physical functions for him: the eating, drinking and defecating mostly, but also the exercising to keep his limbs from atrophying and the general observing of the outside world. And the workers going about their daily rounds in the greenhouse not once noticed the mound of green, cotton-y substance at the foot of the unnamed plant. It was as if a shield of non-being had been set in place to protect him from prying eyes. Whatever it may have been, Bob wasn't once disturbed as the winds continued to howl and the snow piled high against the very panel that had opened to let him in, now very securely in place.

It must have been the renewed heat and vigour of the spring sun that finally made Bob stir. He sat up and pulled away the material around him. His puppy tried to help as well but, even though it yanked for all it was worth, it managed only to get itself more and more entangled till it ended up chasing its own tail and barking madly. Bob laughed and stood up, stretching, his fingers arching upwards as far as they could go. He began to sing, to hum.

"Hey, what's going on in there?" a voice called out from one of the other sections. "There's not supposed to be—"

As the worker in his dirty, brown overalls walked through the door, there was a sudden constriction in his throat. No matter how much he tried, he couldn't get another word out. It was all he could do to stand there in the doorway, staring at Bob the Preacher and his No-Name Puppy like they were apparitions from another world. In fact, Bob looked no different than the first night he had stumbled onto the greenhouse. A little more scruffy, perhaps, and threadbare, but that was it. Nothing had changed in his physical appearance that would cause such a reaction in the worker. And he still wore his insulated coat and seven-league boots, with the greasy tuque pulled low over his forehead.

Bob put his hand on the worker's shoulder as he went by him. Friendly and always smiling, that was Bob the Preacher's way. Even when his message wasn't all that pleasant. Even when it was downright unpalatable. And it usually worked, too—at least for those who allowed themselves to be touched. The worker relaxed visibly and returned Bob's smile.

"May I offer you a cup of coffee?" he asked on regaining his voice. Bob shook his head. "Ah, yes. You're in a hurry?" Bob nodded. "Let me show you the way out, then." He led Bob and the puppy to the front entrance of the greenhouse. "Here we are. It's a beautiful morning, isn't it?" And indeed it was, despite the deformed fish floating belly up along the river's edge and the smog masks that obscured many of the joggers' faces.

"Have a pleasant day. And come back soon, you hear. I make a fresh pot every day."

Not everyone, of course, reacted in the same way when they encountered Bob the Preacher and his puppy strolling down the riverfront path. Some wanted to come closer, to touch his rags. Others recoiled as if in disgust. Women, in particular, steered clear of him, especially those who were of child-bearing age. Bob himself didn't seem to notice either reaction and continued to walk in a leisurely fashion, soaking in the sun and occasionally discarding pieces of his clothing. Only the sound of an explosion behind him caused him to stop for a moment and turn around. What he saw was the top of the greenhouse flying through the air, steel and glass shooting in all directions, as the plants broke out of their imprisonment.

"Ah, now we can breathe," the voice in his head said. "It's springtime for the Earth."

Several of the people who happened to be close to the building when it exploded could now be seen lying on the ground, speared by slivers of glass. But that was no concern of Bob's. There were more important things to do. He was standing next to a shredded maple tree that was struggling to survive in the middle of a gigantic blacktop parking lot. This was where the joggers left their vehicles before hitting the riverfront paths for their morning exercise. It wasn't so much a tree, actually, as a grouping of bare branches about the height of a man. The branches, where they hadn't been snapped by children, ravaged by ice, or scorched by car exhaust fumes, were covered with a thin layer of soot. In other words, a tree not even fit for insects to gnaw on.

After gently brushing away the soot, Bob found one or two buds, just tiny bumps really against the bark. But it meant the tree was alive, if only barely. Bob placed his hand on the living branch, feeling the feeble pulse, the shrivelled roots sucking away at PCB-enriched nourishment. Suddenly, the tree shot into the air, zooming up twenty metres or more without hesitation. Its trunk thickened to two metres in diameter. A dense canopy of leaves arched out in a perfectly symmetrical circle with a radius of ten metres. From its base, the ground undulated. The asphalt cracked open, shaking off the parked cars like ants and hurling some into the river before covering the entire area with a thick, undulating carpet of dandelions and chicory plants.

The whole time, Bob and his puppy stood beneath it, either unaware of or ignoring the screams of those who had witnessed the transformation. And, just as swiftly as it had begun, it was over. Now, there was absolute silence, perhaps for the first time ever—but definitely not the last. Birds alighted in the branches without the least chirp. Squirrels ran up the trunk on tip-toe. A fish leaped out of the water for a glass-eyed look, then noiselessly dove back in.

Humans started to gather around, though making sure to stay well outside the perimeter of the maple's shade, which somehow always remained a perfectly symmetrical circle, no matter where the sun happened to be. Bob put his hand on the trunk, fingertips on bark. As he made contact, his voice rang out for all to hear—and yet no one in the steadily thickening crowd once saw him open his mouth.

"My name is Bob the Preacher," he said in his awful, silent way. "Heed my words if you wish to save the Earth from total annihilation. I am not the saviour, no. I'm just a poor hobo. But I can show you how *you* can save the Earth before it's too late. Heed my words. There are powerful forces behind me. They're angry at what you've done, at the destruction you've set in motion in so short a stewardship. But they're willing to give you a chance to set it right, to save yourselves. They also know that you don't believe something just because someone tells you so. So, they're willing to give you a sample of their terrible power. Watch the news tonight, and you'll see what I mean. Thank you."

With that, the voice stopped. And the spell was broken. Suddenly, the silence was replaced by the sound of sirens and the screeching of tires. Policemen with cattle prods ordered the crowd to disperse. One of them, a bulked-up young man wearing an opaque visor, approached Bob the Preacher with the obvious intention of arresting him for disturbing the peace.

"Hey, you," he said. "What do you think you're doing? Public speaking without a permit is strictly against the law. Sorry, but I'm gonna have to take you in."

But, the moment he tried to pass the line between shadow and light, he was sent bouncing back, reeling to the ground.

"Shit!" he said, holding his bloodied nose.

"I'm sorry," the voice said. "You can't enter. It's forbidden for humans to enter the area reserved for Bob the Preacher and his No-Name Puppy."

"What the fuck are you talking about, scumbag!" The policeman yelled. "I'll enter where the fuck I want." But the policeman's second attempt to penetrate the tree's canopy was just as unsuccessful as the first. At this point, he unholstered his gun and aimed it at the scabby-looking vagabond's head. "Come out, asshole. And be quick about it. Otherwise, I'll wipe that fucking smile off your face for good."

"The news at six," the voice said, ignoring the policeman. "Tune into the news."

The policeman fired. Fortunately for him, the ricocheting bullet whizzed right by his head. One of the bystanders, a young mother pushing a baby carriage, wasn't so lucky. She dropped to the ground in a pool of blood, clutching at her chest as the carriage continued across the street on its own.

"Please don't fire again," the voice said. "You might injure someone else."

"Don't you fucking try to tell me what to fucking do!" the policeman shouted, the gun shaking in his hand as his face flamed red. "You're in no position to give orders. Now, either you come out of there this instant or I call the riot squad—and those motherfuckers will blow you to kingdom come before you can stick a thumb up your stinking arse."

The policeman was true to his word. The riot squad came, grim, death-masked, bristling with the latest crowd-control weaponry and AI-guided armaments. And, cutting a swath through the citizenry, they surrounded the tree, formed *un cordon sanitaire* around it, as much to keep the surging crowds away as to prevent Bob the Preacher from escaping. But Bob had no intention of fleeing. He just sat beneath the tree, waiting. Those looking on saw only a middle-aged man dressed in rags and, next to him, his even scruffier dog. What they didn't realize was that he was in constant communion with his spirits and knew, minute by minute, what was going on throughout the world.

"The news you have been waiting so anxiously for has arrived," the voice said to the crowd at precisely six p.m. "See it for yourselves."

No one needed a TV screen for this news. An image appeared in the sky. First, the face of a woman, an announcer, all out of breath. She could hardly speak for her excitement, hardly get the words out:

> Toronto is a calm city tonight. After more than 100 years of constant shelling, the rockets, the mortars, the submachine guns are quiet. How is this possible? How did it happen? No one knows. The various leaders are in emergency session at this very moment, refusing to answer any questions.

This was followed by scenes of the city itself, mostly rubble by now, and the surrounding area. It was a sight to make arms manufacturers and dealers head for the nearest high-rise window. It seemed that every rocket launcher, every bazooka and mortar battery, every machine gun, rifle and pistol had been encircled by vines. Soldiers, rebels, snipers could barely take aim before a vine sprang up and seized their weapons. And it was no use trying to hack them free. Those hacking, stabbing, slicing weapons were immobilized as well.

Slowly, right before the very eyes of the world, Toronto was restored to its former glory. Every trace of the civil war was erased in a matter of minutes as the buildings rose from the dust, the roads repaired themselves and the streetlights came to life. No, it wasn't just restored to its former glory. In the days to come, it became an even more beautiful city, a veritable garden where life's struggle no longer concerned the inhabitants. And there were trees and shrubs everywhere, the air thick with the fragrance of flowers and fruits. It was as if the people of Toronto were being rewarded for the years of misery, the decades of living like frightened rats in tunnels beneath the ground.

But, even if the puzzled natives of the city were more than pleased with the sudden upturn in their fortunes, the sentiment was in no way universal. Already, in various capitals around the world, there were rumblings of a deep conspiracy. While politicians and military leaders pointed fingers and thumped bargaining tables, scientists went about proclaiming the impossibility of such an event, how it went against all the laws of nature, how energy couldn't just be created out of nothing, how entropy had to be served and couldn't be so arbitrarily reversed.

And then some of them, not scientists really but ad executives experienced in such things, quickly came up with a theory. Mass hypnosis, the same phenomenon that had brought them Nazi America. Their theory was that Toronto hadn't changed at all—only people's perception of it. The same with the man sitting under a maple tree. All we have to do, the ad-exec-scientists explained, is ignore it and go about our business. After all, illusions can only hurt if you believe them. And, though some felt in their hearts that the theory was flawed in some way, that's what most of the humans did, blithely bypassing Bob the Preacher and Toronto, the city that could have been a splendid tribute to a new consciousness.

"These humans are ingenious in their ingenuousness," the voices said. "They have as much inner armour as outer. It's time we show them that we mean business."

"Business?" Bob the Preacher said, feeling a bit queasy, especially after his puppy howled and tried to bury its head. "What do you mean by that?"

"Yes. It's time to give them a taste of what we can really do. Tell us, Bob. You, as a former human, should know. Where are the worst atrocities being committed in the world today?"

Bob fidgeted. He felt somewhat like a traitor, a quisling. Besides, there were so many atrocities, injustices and both natural and unnatural disasters, he really didn't know where to start: Indigenous peoples on display in cages around the world, the poor and inner city homeless being deliberately culled and marked for elimination, scions of the utterly wealthy kidnapping asexuals for their off-Earth orgies.

"Well," he said at last. "You've got your choice, really. Just about anywhere but Toronto right now."

"Hmm," the voices said thoughtfully. "Those are all good, all worthy of redress. But it's not quite what we want."

"I was reading a magazine—"

"Yes!" the voices exclaimed, trembling with excitement. "We have it! That's it! Off you go."

And, as they said that, Bob the Preacher found himself not sitting quietly beneath a maple tree but scrambling up the side of an excavation in a torrential rain, loaded down with a sackful of crushed rocks and desperately trying to pull himself up a rickety rope ladder. He paused to look around. There were thousands of others in the pit with him, all covered in thick mud. Some were scaling the ladders that seemed never-ending in the mist; others were several hundred metres below, rushing about at the bottom of the pit. And this wasn't the only pit. The vast area was pockmarked with them, like giant pus-holes on the face of the Earth.

He could see that not all the men would make it out of those pits alive, that some had already drowned or been crushed beneath the weight of their loads. A whip cracked above his head and there were shouts for him to move along. With the last of his strength, he managed to climb over the top of the pit. There, a man in a yellow slicker immediately pointed a gun at him and directed him to a pile of well-guarded earth, where he was told to dump his load. Some of the earth glittered as he spilled it out of his sack. High above, a man with a gold pinkie ring floated over the ground in a covered sedan chair. Bob made his way back to the pit. As he slowly descended the ladder, he spoke to the others, to the thousands who laboured away, not just in this pit but in all of them at once.

"You are destroying me," his voice said, in a tone that forced them to lay down their picks and listen. "You are cutting me to pieces—and for what? For earth that glitters. You are digging away the foundations, tearing out the roots. My trees are sinking into oblivion. Their giant carcasses rotting in your acid rain. The waters . . . the polluted waters are rolling in . . . flooding . . . drowning in carbon dioxide. My forest has run out of air to breathe. It can no longer feed its million billion mouths. But no more. It has gone too far. Lay down your picks for good. Abandon your futile labours. Walk away now. Or suffer the consequences."

But, even as he said it, Bob knew that the listening was only temporary. Oh, one or two of the men did have the nerve to walk away, but they were quickly gunned down, and their bodies tossed back into the pit. The rest looked at one another for a moment, and then, at the crack of a whip, returned to work. Bob found himself back beneath his maple tree. He was crying, and his puppy was licking his face, doing its best to comfort him, to convince him that what was about to happen was necessary.

"Let me try again," Bob pleaded, ever the kind-hearted preacher. "I know I can get them to listen. Please. Deep down, these are good people."

The voices didn't answer. Instead, bodies began to pop up in the grass around the tree. Partly buried in the ground, only their heads and shoulders showing, these bodies were nevertheless still alive—for the moment. Some were screaming in awful torment as their skulls were emptied by ever-busy insects, leaving the tongues for last. Others never got over the shock and died in silence, using their last moments to reflect on what might have been. In an effort to save them, policemen and paramedics ran about the grass trying to pull them out of the ground. Their bodies came away in pieces. So, when saving them didn't work, the police tried to put a quick end to their misery. They shot them, crushed their heads like rotten watermelons, ran them over with their cars and paddy wagons.

At the start of the carnage, Bob the Preacher had lowered his eyes. But that hadn't kept him from witnessing every last bit of it, reflected inside his head. He even recognized some of the bodies—especially one in a yellow slicker and another who, before being devoured alive by centipedes, disgorged a gold pinkie ring.

> I didn't want any flowers, I only wanted
> To lie with my hands turned up and be utterly empty.

"That's no longer possible," the voices said. "We must prove that what we do is no illusion."

In a matter of minutes, the thousands of bodies had started to decompose. The stench was awful, driving away even the hardiest spectator. Many of the riot policemen, ordered to remain at their posts, fainted despite their gas masks. The stench rose as a cloud and settled over the city. It penetrated to the very pores. There was no escaping it, leaving the inhabitants to hang over their toilet bowls.

Later that very same day, someone in authority stood before Bob the Preacher. She wore an asbestos and anti-radiation suit and talked through a loudspeaker.

"Who are you?" she asked in a forceful way designed to get answers. "What do you want from us?"

"I'm Bob the Preacher. I'm here to save the Earth if you'll let me. Have you the authority?"

"You call this saving the Earth," she said, her face twisting. "It's murder, pure and simple."

"Some must die so that others can live. Today, the rain forest is healthy again. The mines have been filled in. The trees are upright, their roots reaching deep into the earth, secure. There is peace."

"What bloody well gives you the right to decide when peace comes or not?" She stabbed her finger repeatedly towards him. "Were you elected?"

"Elected? Is that what you call it? The elected ones? Perhaps, so. A long time ago."

"Well, let me tell you something, buster. You weren't elected by me. Or by anyone else around here. We run a democratic system in this country. So, no one tells us what to do. Neither you nor your Arab dictator friends. They're behind all this, aren't they? I should've known. They're the only ones with the money. What do they want? A monopoly on the world's energy."

"We are democratic, too. Our 'Arab dictator friends' were given neither more nor less than you—just an equal portion of the bodies. After all, they're just as guilty."

"Guilty! Of course, they're guilty. But what's that got to do with us?"

"This is fruitless. You humans have a well-honed penchant for blaming others for your problems. Passing the buck, I believe you call it."

"I'll show you what we have a penchant for, you shit-corroded pile of rags!" she screamed. "If you don't come out from under that tree within the hour, we're going to hit you with everything we got. Everything! Do you understand? And let me tell you, I damn well have the authority."

The woman in authority meant what she said. When Bob the Preacher hadn't emerged in the allotted time, the heavy-duty lasers moved in. Crackling with blue lightning, they raked him and the tree full blast: from above, from straight ahead and from below. Not one ray got through. Then, after a fifteen-minute warning to the residents, they dropped a low-level radiation device that destroyed a good portion of that part of the city and the surrounding countryside, leaving dark shadows against any of the buildings that still stood.

But Bob the Preacher, his puppy, the tree and its shadow remained untouched. Finally, they hit it with their most powerful fusion bomb, as yet untested under actual conditions of war. The island vanished, the rivers around it dried up, the sky turned black, radiation poisoning spread over a radius of several hundred kilometres. Still the little green oasis floated, unharmed in the midst of so much destruction. Even then, however, the humans didn't give up. They continued to drop bomb after bomb on it, hoping to deplete its energy supply, to find the weakness in it, the fatal flaw. For they knew nothing that didn't have some flaw, a way for entropy to sneak in.

"These humans are a tenacious bunch," the voices said with what seemed a hint of admiration. "It almost makes you want to leave them be on their path to absolute destruction, let them fall off the edge, dragging everything else with them. But we can't do that, can we? Wait a minute! Perhaps if we give them a little taste of it, just a tiny feel for that total annihilation, they might finally relent, might finally admit the *mea culpa* of their actions. Bob, it's time to do your duty again. Sound the warning. Let them know we, too, mean business."

Amid the almost constant thunderclap of atomic bombs and the remote-controlled robotic devices hurling themselves with pre-programmed ferocity against the tree, Bob spoke out once again. This time, however, his voice was weary and the sadness in it was unmistakable.

"Humans," he said, the voice, though it quavered and faltered, penetrating to the very depths of their fallout shelters, to the bored-out mountains, to the ever-circling shark-nosed submarines, to the insect-like drones. "I'm to inform you that the Earth is ready to withdraw its bounty from you, to buck you off its broad back. It has fed and nourished you faithfully until now, even while you were stabbing it repeatedly, even while you were tearing out her very womb. It has supported every atrocity, every act of violence, and each time it has come back stronger than ever, with renewed vigour. But this is it. No more. *Nada*. Let us demonstrate."

And with that, every blade of grass, every stalk of corn, every sheath of grain, every vine, every bush and every tree —every tree but one, that is—vanished from the face of the Earth. Just as the bodies had come shooting out, the plants slipped in. Gone, disappeared without a trace. It was a scene that should make us shudder to this day, so many lifetimes removed that even those who keep track have lost track. No desert could be so desolate and cold. No lifeless moon so barren. No polished skull so empty.

"Until you come to your senses," the voice said, "this is the way it shall be. We are sure it won't be long, though. At least, we hope not."

For a while, it seemed the voices were right. Not long after the Earth withdrew its bounty, the leaders of the humans called for a truce—and talks. They were willing to discuss the conditions laid down.

"Ah," the voices said to Bob, "this must make you exceedingly glad. We will have peace at last."

For the first time in a very long time Bob allowed himself a smile, albeit a tiny one. His faith in the human ability to adapt had nearly vanished during that period. Now, they were finally coming to their senses.

"We have chosen you to conduct the talks for us," the voices told him. "A team of human negotiators will be flown in presently. We will not ask for much, just a sharing of the Earth among equals. We don't want slaves, just as humans don't want to be slaves. We want only continuity."

The team of human negotiators consisted of three. Among them—nay, leading them—Bob recognized the woman in authority, the one who had threatened him and had ordered the unleashing of so much death and destruction. Now, she came wearing her diplomatic peace cap and carrying a bouquet of artificial flowers in her hands.

"Greetings," Bob said, as he lowered the energy shield around the tree to allow them in. "It's a pleasure to see that humans haven't lost their age-old instinct for survival. And that they're still capable of solving problems in a peaceful way. Now, where shall we begin?"

"By getting rid of you!" the woman screamed.

And she yanked one of the fake flowers, blowing herself and everyone within a kilometre radius sky-high. Everyone, that is, except Bob, his No-Name Puppy and the tree. All three came floating gently back to Earth—or whatever was left of it.

"That does it," the voices said. "When we're through with them, they'll come crawling to us. They'll be willing to do anything. They'll volunteer to be our pets, to clean out our intestines, to inhabit the recesses of our anal tracts."

But, one more time, the voices hadn't anticipated, hadn't counted on, the stubbornness—and never-say-die resourcefulness—of the human animal. In the midst of mass starvation and turmoil, in the midst of general cannibalism and slaughter, of diaspora and social collapse, some survived. They survived by producing food through genetic manipulation, by imitating the very plants themselves in their high-tech labs. Vegetation was created out of desktops, out of the decomposing bodies of the less fortunate, out of shoestrings and hockey sticks. Everything that could be converted to food was—for those with the means to pay for it.

"This is ridiculous," the voices said in exasperation. "Bob, we don't know what to do. Instead of admitting they were wrong, instead of trying a new way, a way that would be best for all of us, these humans would rather fight to the death. They would rather pile up their dead in our path, their billions upon billions slaughtered—and for what reason? Is what we offer them so bad? No, they want dominion or nothing. What are we going to do, Bob? Look, they're mocking us. They're hiding behind their armour. Aren't they a pretty sight? Bob, what would you have us do?"

But Bob the Preacher wasn't listening. Bob was crying. He was in mourning for his species, for all the innocents that had been destroyed and for the many more yet to come, for those who would have envisioned a different world if only they'd been given the chance, and for those who were stubborn and proud and stupid enough to hold out until the end—even if they knew they were wrong. He was also in mourning because he realized there was nothing more he could do. The decision had already been made and their fate sealed. The genetically engineered food would turn to poison in their mouths—and they would fall by the wayside, each and every last one of them, their faces like death masks pressed against the vacuum-sealed glass. Then the Earth would be meticulously re-constructed: the jungles, the rivers, the mountains, the timber wolves, the puppies, the insects.

"And a few humans," Bob said, with a hint of hope. "Don't forget a few human beings. After all, they created the cities and the books. They're not all bad, you know. Besides, they would be a great way to top off your re-built world, wouldn't they? Admit it. They're the finest thing in all of creation, the crowning glory."

"If they can't live with us," the voices answered rever-berating with sternness, with a collective shaking of their heads, "we are better off without them."

The last scene in this tale takes place on a beach facing one of the Earth's great oceans. The water is warm and silky, teeming with new life. The sun emits exactly the right amount of light and heat, without any dangerous radiation. Lying on the beach, the gentle waves lapping against her legs, is a woman. A young woman wearing nothing but a ratty cashmere sweater. Sitting beside her is Bob the Preacher and his No-Name Puppy. After a few moments, the woman is roused from what seems an ageless sleep.

"Who am I?" she says, yawning, stretching, shading her eyes from the sun.

"You're the last human being on Earth," Bob says aloud, his own voice sounding exceedingly strange to him.

"But that can't be," she says. "Why, look. You're here."

"Not really."

"No," she says, touching his arm. "No riddles. You're a man. I'm a woman. A man and a woman were put on Earth to make children. We must make children. That can't be denied."

"I suppose not," Bob says.

"Then, let's get to it!"

And with that, she pulls off his few remaining rags and brings him down on her, lowers him onto her. He does everything a man must do, culminating in a rabid spurting as she wraps her legs around him for better penetration. Afterwards, he rolls away, hiding his face. It's only then that the woman notices something strange between her legs. The water lapping against them, touching the vaginal cavity, is turning a darkly-foliated shade of green.

"What's that?" she screams, rubbing herself and waving the green-tinted hand before his eyes. "What have you done to me? What have you filled me with?"

"I told you I wasn't a man. I've filled you with the green fuse of life. That's all I can do."

"You bastard! You fucking traitor! You twisted freak! I don't want any green fuse. I want babies. I want humans to reclaim their rightful place. Right next to the gods. If you can't give me that, then fuck you. May you be cursed for all eternity. May you be remembered down through the ages as the man who did away with human beings, his own flesh and blood."

And, saying that, she grows old and shrivels, weeping for all the children she'll never have. Above her, a rocket trails smoke through the sky, signalling perhaps the end of a species. Or the start of something new.

The water I taste is warm and salt, like the sea,
And comes from a country far away as health.

Bob the Preacher can feel the hard tug within him, the ebb and flow of the blood. He thinks back on that corrosive winter day when it all started, when Robert the Hobo fell through a wall panel into the heat and the vision of a greenhouse where a unique symbiosis took place. At the same time, he can feel the human in him returning, and that makes him hurt even more. It manifests itself as a state of confusion that causes him to hold his head—just like that first time when he grovelled on the floor of an abandoned library, hoping one of the marble blocks would detach itself and put him out of his misery. But before he can get too far, before he can re-activate the mechanisms that'll have him back as Robert the Hobo, his lovable, friendly No-Name Puppy jumps on his chest and, wagging its tail excitedly, slits his throat with a razor-sharp nail, neatly from ear to ear.

Since it was my turn for story-telling and since no one's exempt from the duty, I chose the tale of how the Earth was saved from total and utter destruction by Bob the Preacher and his No-Name Puppy —both of whom can be seen at least for the time being, deeply-rooted and well-nourished at last, next to the perfectly symmetrical maple.

Now that The Sleepers have returned and are on the verge of landing at the edge of Forest Earth, I hope the story hasn't caused offence to anyone. I offer it not as an object lesson but as a sign of forgiveness, as a signal that things may turn out differently this time around. And, if they don't, well . . . There may be those among us who would fault you, Mother, for what they feel is about to befall us, for a renewed uncertainty that may never be set right. There are those who may say you could have prevented it—if you had so wished. That you could have secured our future, and the Earth's, for time immemorial. But who can blame you for feeling pity? Who can blame you for showing mercy? Who can blame you for not destroying every single human being after all, for allowing those pathetic few to escape? No one can fight their own nature, can they, Mother Yggdrasil, Great Tree of Life? No one. Not even you.

—

Hothouse Love previously published in *Paradise Island and Other Galaxies* (Exile Editions, 2020).

SAVING MORRO

Cora Siré

I first spotted him standing on the shoulder just outside of town. Normally, I don't pick up hitchhikers. It's just too risky, especially what with my camper and everything I've got on board. Better outfitted than most roamers, I am. Makes me a target in some places. I've seen the water vultures in these parts, roaming in packs of big-wheelers and greedy chrome. I'd just left the hide-a-bar where, to put it mildly, I wasn't exactly offered the red-carpet treatment. Glowering stares from under those corp-gov caps: Potashville writ large. Buncha men staring down a woman, not a courteous soul among them. I tried to get a chinwag or two going, but they didn't have the time of afternoon for me. One shot of contraband, and I was back in my camper, feeling not humbled exactly. Just, I don't know, disenchanted.

After picking up Arden the hitchhiker, and, much later when he finally opened his mouth, the chilly reception in the hide-a-bar with its pitchers of illegal beer fell into place. I swear I'd even heard the glassy music of ice cubes being scooped from somewhere under the counter. Haven't heard that sound in, what? Over a decade? What Arden eventually told me about Potashville proves there's a reason for most things, right? Cause and effect. Although this whole situation with Arden has me confounded. All his muttering and groaning on the cot back there. "Morro, Morro," he keeps saying, trying to force me to come to a decision.

But back when I was pulling out of the hide-a-bar's parking lot, I was a bit pissed about it all, and, okay, I admit it, starved for company. So, I saw this lanky guy, kind of like a stretched-out praying mantis, standing on the shoulder of the eastbound ramp. No cardboard sign or anything, but he had his thumb out.

"Where you heading?"

"East," he said.

Well, obviously.

I commanded the passenger door to open, and he climbed in. "Put this on," I said. The harness disengaged from the roof. The guy was so skinny, he had to adjust it, fiddling with the keypad until it was on tight. His hands were shaking, and he just looked so dried up. Half my age by the look of his green eyes, but not an ounce of juice to him.

"I'm heading towards Brandon," I said. "After that it's north all the way to Thompson." I didn't get into the logistics at that point—the fact that my battery would need recharging pretty soon, that I planned to overnight somewhere after crossing provincial lines, well before Brandon.

"Name's Fray," I said. "What's yours?"

"Arden."

I asked him if he lived in Esterhazy, and he nodded, saying nothing more as my dash informed me, once again, that the place was now called Potashville. "So what?" I yelled. "Just get us to Brandon and mind your own business." The onboard voice system was the bane of my existence. Couldn't live without it, couldn't stand the interventions. I guess Arden found my tone a little aggressive. He kind of cringed and looked out the window. He was wearing faded-green fatigues, a long-sleeved shirt and pants, sensible considering the sunlight in these parts. On his feet, a pair of boots like the kind miners wear. Steel-toed or whatever.

"You a miner?"

"No."

Not much of a talker either. I wanted to ask him about the town formerly known as Esterhazy, a name I always liked. Sounds like a person, right? Esther Hazy. Potash capital of the world, producing the stuff used to make fertilizer for all those industrial farming complexes taking over the globe. Renamed Potashville. One of those corp-gov towns now, run by a cartel in return for hectares of land, unlimited access to utilities, and more or less freed of any regulations having to do with quality of human life. It was only later, when Arden finally opened up, that I learned the extent of the misery inflicted on residents.

An AmaZonia freighter barrelled past on the tracks alongside the highway. It was going at least twice the speed of my camper's fifty kph limit, with train cars strung far as the eye could see. Loaded with water, most likely, along with a regiment of armed security, too. Arden shuddered at the sight of it. I could smell his desperation.

I released my harness and crawled to the back of the camper for my secret stash. I was still on my guard, didn't trust him entirely, kept glancing back at him on his seat even though his harness prevented him from turning around. I crept past my cot, underneath which I stored my canisters, opened the hidden panel just above the back wheels, and reached in for one of the A-Dh lozenges I'd stockpiled in Lithiumton, back when they were still handing them out for free. Worth their weight in rare-earth metals now. As I was crawling back to the driver's seat, the camper veered right, kicking up dust on the shoulder, “Obstacle, Obstacle!” bleating from the dash. Arden panicked. “Hey, we’re going off the highway.”

On the centre lane, a real vulture was pecking at what was left of a carcass, gopher or prairie dog, most likely. I told Arden not to worry, that the camper would right itself momentarily, which it soon did.

“I’m not used to these self-driving cars,” he said. “Or vans, or whatever this . . . .”

“It’s a 2031 Buzz,” I said. “You know, the VW bus first introduced in the ’20s. Modelled after the original hipster version my parents crossed the continent in way back before you and I were born. Same colour orange, by the way, though not as boho chic. But this one’s solid, seven years old now, and I’ve added some special features.” I could’ve talked up my camper for hours, but Arden didn’t seem that interested. Along with tremors and fatigue, severe dehydration could cause indifference, so I didn’t take it personally.

I handed him the lozenge. “Let it melt slowly. I mean, don’t chew it or anything. It’ll jack up your fluids.” Eventually. Anti-dehydration pharmaceuticals being a work in progress.

Arden stared at the lozenge for a moment, then painstakingly unwrapped the trademark aqua-blue-and-white striped packaging. His hands were shaking so bad. “I’ve heard of these,” he said. “Not available around here. Do you have a lot of them?”

“Nope,” I lied and pointed to a receptacle below the dash for the wrapping. “That’s for trash.”

I settled back in my seat, checked the settings. The battery would hold up for another eighty kilometres or so. Arden’s knee jittered away. “You never mentioned where you’re heading exactly,” I said.

“To the big lake. Down east.”

“Winnipeg? Superior?”

“Yeah, one of those.”

I told him that when I first became a roamer, I spent a couple of summers out near Kenora. "Zillions of lakes in the area and lots of good campsites. Shade, too. That's all I needed at the time." Not true, really. I was lonely as fuck back then. Not used to this nomadic existence. My first summer there, I stumbled upon a campground that was a hoot. Lots of singles like me, some families with kids.

One June night as I was collecting rainwater during a rare downpour, a guy volunteered to help me load the canisters into my camper. Chavez was strong and in no time, I'd replenished my water supply, with extras strapped onto the roof. I made him coffee, and we sat under the dripping spruce trees, watching the stars re-emerge as the storm cleared, our T-shirts air-drying in the warm night. He'd come up from New Mexico, and had lots of stories to tell, as did I. Then he played his ukulele, strumming to improvised mashups. "Don't go chasing waterfalls" segueing into "Fire and Rain" and "A Hard Rain's A-Gonna Fall" (my late granddad's shower songs), and "Here Comes the Rain Again" (as if!) and "Umbrella" (where are you now, Rihanna?) closing with the ditzy "Raindrops Keep Falling on My Head," which cracked me up. We just clicked, and that night, when Chavez leaned in and tugged on my braid, "Fray?" to the sweet smells of pine trees and rain, I couldn't say no.

Of course, I didn't mention that Chavez had the same curly hair and wide green-eyed look as Arden. Aside from that, they're utterly different. The main factor being resilience. Chavez had been through a lot, his big hands nicked with scars, but he kept moving forward, didn't dwell on the past. Me neither. Hell, I can hardly remember much of my pre-roamer life. No room for nostalgia that way. Although I did feel a tug when I told Arden about my follies, how I followed Chavez back east, then south, where he claimed we'd be better off in the winter. "Never listen to a poet," I said. Arden laughed, a sure sign the lozenge was kicking in.

After all the solo travelling, it was like a dam had burst, that's how starved I was for conversation. I have to say this about Arden: once the lozenge worked its magic, he was an attentive listener.

Those were miserable months in Nashville, me and Chavez lining up at food banks along with all the other migrants that winter of 2034. The town overflowed with people from seawater-flooded Florida and the hurricaned Carolinas. Others hailed from burnt-out Colorado, droughty Nebraska, Iowa and Kansas, along with stranded snowbirds from Chicago, Toledo and Cleveland. It felt like everyone converged inland into Tennessee.

Chavez hooked up with some indie musicians, spent the nights rehearsing and chasing I don't know what. Not waterfalls, that's for sure. Come spring, I decided to head back north, and he decided he had no better ideas than to try to "make it in Nashville." That worn-out dream doesn't seem to dry up, no matter how much the planet does.

The morning I left Nashville, Chavez tugged my braid for the last time. He handed me a big old bag full of food, a selfless gesture I will never forget. My trip back north took me close to a year. Long lineups at recharging stations, reservoirs and food distributors, but by June, I was back at the site near Kenora, right where I'd started.

Then came the water riots of 2035, and, wouldn't you know it, the entire area surrounding all Great Lakes and peripheral communities was seized by the cartel. AmaZonia evicted all temporary residents, shutdown the campsites, introduced checkpoints and border controls. There was gang warfare among the water vultures, and I learned how to keep my head low and avoid them as I headed west, my heart more than a little chipped, but my resolve intact. Made a pact with myself never to get attached like that, never to linger too long in one place. I skipped the part about the pact, but I told Arden about the situation around Lake Superior, how he might as well forget about getting anywhere near the water. "The whole place is under corp-gov control."

"Sounds like Potashville," he said.

"But way bigger."

We passed a wind farm, acres and acres of what must've once been soya and cornfields. From columns of towering turbines, mechanical arms sliced the sky like an army of recruits in formation standing on the scorched earth of Saskatchewan.

Arden's trembling had subsided, his face was getting some colour even around those prominent cheekbones, and his lips didn't look quite so grey. Just when we were about to cross into Manitoba, the dash flashed a moisture warning, *Rainfall, Rainfall.* I directed the steering to pull into a scraggly field.

"We're in luck, Arden."

He fumbled with his harness and jumped outside while I unloaded the canisters in a race against time. Who knew how long the rain would last?

Arden stood there with his arms and face raised to receive the droplets like the manna from heaven they were. A beautiful moment to behold, but I needed his help, and corralled him into flipping open the lids while I positioned the canisters alongside the camper so our heavy lifting would be minimal. Once that was done, I said, "Okay, do your rain dance or whatever." I pulled the elastics off my braids and shook them out. I couldn't even remember when I'd last washed my hair.

Meanwhile, Arden unbuttoned and flung off his shirt, letting gushers wash over his bony torso and face. But after his momentary joy, he doubled over and fell onto the field. Bam. His green shirt lay next to him like a lifeless rag. I caught sight of a tattoo on his bare back: the words "Great Forest" over a tree whose leafy branches formed a green fist emerging from a trunk-like wrist.

I ran, flipped his body over, and slapped his wet face. He came to and sat up, kneading the calf of his bent leg, forehead on his knee. The short-lived bliss of warm rain dripping through my hair was superseded by the realization that Arden was fast becoming a liability. *The pact, Fray, remember the pact.*

The wind came up, whistling across the field, a lone tree-skeleton bending over a dilapidated fence in the distance. I knew that wind. It meant the rain clouds would move on, dissipated as so often happens in extreme heat. I threw Arden his shirt and started pouring the half-filled canisters into each other, loading the full ones back into the camper. I kept one aside and brought it over to Arden along with a mug and told him to take a few good drinks. A farewell gift. I'd made up my mind.

He dipped the mug into the liquid, brought it to his mouth, and I swear there were tears in his eyes, new self-produced tears, not just the leftover traces of rain on his face. His body was so dry as to be like a sponge. It takes more than a half an hour of moisture exposure to counter chronic dehydration and its symptoms. Low blood volume and pressure from the lack of oxygen in his body and the risk of hypovolemic shock. Not to mention the other nasty symptoms: leg cramps, fainting, seizures, kidney failure, dizziness, confusion. The guy was a walking time bomb. I had to get rid of him.

I got into the camper. The battery levels had just enough juice to make another forty kilometres to the recharge station in Griswold. I locked the doors, powered the engine, and keyed in the driving instructions. The camper shifted then stopped. "Obstruction, Obstruction." Arden's face looked at me outside the passenger window. His hand on the door, trying to open it. There was such a look on his face, like in a second he'd be ready to smash the window if I didn't let him in. I shook my head, mouthed the words, Sorry, gotta move on. Arden hit the window, as expected. Shatterproof glass, it wouldn't break. But his hand would. Fuck it. I let him in.

Neither of us spoke for a while. Arden was mulling things over, and I didn't like how his hands were rubbing the thighs of his damp pants, like he was cooking up a plan. Half-baked no doubt, involving carjacking the camper (good luck with the security system), knocking me out (not a chance), stealing my supplies.

"I'm sorry, Fray," he finally said.

"For what?" Now, upon reflection, I can see how Arden might've been apologizing in advance for what he was concocting to do to me.

Terrible planner, considering he's the one lying on the cot back there, muttering about saving Morro. Leaving me at this crossroad. As in go east as planned and dump Arden at a clinic in Brandon, or go back to the hellhole with him onboard? I command the camper to pull a U-ey and head towards the sinking sun. Maybe because all along, as a roamer, no matter how self-sufficient I try to be, it's the selfless gestures here and there that've kept me going. You can't always be on the receiving end, can you? Sometimes you have to give back the mercy, even if it's more than risky.

But three hours ago, I was still clinging to what you might call the new morality of this parched world. Like those instructions onboard the last plane I took, sometime in the late '20s. Put the oxygen mask on your face first. "You can get out in Griswold," I said.

"I want to go back."

"To Potashville?"

"I have to go back."

"Why'd you leave in the first place?"

"It's a long story."

"Try me." I figured it'd provide me with some entertainment for the next hour. And it did. But not the good kind. More on the harrowing side, and I've heard lots of tragedies in my years as a roamer.

Arden scratched his head like he didn't know where to begin. "Something happened last night. I just can't leave them behind."

"Who?"

"Got a baby back in Potashville, me and my partner, Jesse. They're not doing well."

I'd been uncomfortable since after the rain dance incident. Alarm bells went off in my head. What had Arden done last night?

"Ever since she gave birth to Morro, Jesse's been off work. And you don't get water rations in Potashville if you're not working." Arden was warming up, kept talking, kinda incoherently, but I pieced things together.

The long and short of his story was that the baby's bouts of fevers and diarrhea and her ensuing dehydration had depleted the family's water supply. "We were down to a few drops." Arden hatched a plan to steal some water. Arden was a fork-lift operator, and as an employee of the corporation, he had access to the properties—the mines, bunkers and warehouses where, surprise, surprise, the company stored mega-vats of the water delivered by AmaZonia Rail. The tons and tons of water needed for potash mining. Along with a good portion allocated to the executives' personal use in a compound created for the top brass. I'd seen the same thing in Lithiumton, the hectares patrolled by drones and all that electric fencing surrounding fancy houses, wooded parklands, even fountains—an unimaginable cruelty considering the chronic thirst and skyrocketing infant mortality.

Last night, Arden stole into the warehouse with the idea of siphoning off a few canisters-worth of water for his baby Morro and partner. When a truck pulled in for a load of water, Arden waited it out, killing his headlights, then followed the truck, figuring that it was going somewhere more remote and conducive to his heist. The truck drove into a high-security zone. Soon, past the fencing, the flatland became so green, it looked to be almost fluorescent even at night.

Arden witnessed the nozzles retract from the truck body and the slow, methodical watering of eighteen long greens, beautifully landscaped with trees, flower patches, ponds and waterfalls, where the corporates spent their spare hours. "I'd never seen a golf course before. But I knew that if they're withholding water from children just so they can have some fun on the weekends, we don't stand a chance." He drove home in his pickup and formulated a plan B.

"I gave my last ration coupon to Jesse, told her to drive to the reservoir with Morro, that I'd be back soon. I started walking down to the highway. It took me hours to make the exit ramp where you picked me up. If I don't bring water within a day or two, Morro's going to die. Maybe Jesse, too, if not of thirst, then heartbreak." Arden looked at me. "As soon as you recharge, drive me back there. Please?"

He didn't know how much water I had onboard, beyond the canisters we'd just collected. I had more than enough to make it up to Le Pas, maybe even Thompson. Lots of lakes up there, and my pump and filter were state of the art. Bought them in Nelson before crossing the border into New United Alberta.

I didn't entirely believe Arden at this point. Tried to punch holes in his story. Like how he got in and out of the so-called golf course undetected by drones and security. How his pick-up could run for that long without solar power of daylight. I asked if his house was air-conditioned, he said yes.

"So your baby isn't burning up?"

"As long as she doesn't get another fever."

"Does your partner have family in that hellhole?"

Arden said there were two brothers, both working in the mine.

"They'll take care of her and the baby."

"I doubt it," he said.

While we were talking I kept thinking about those damn ice cubes at the bar, the sounds—like evil wind chimes—when the bartender scooped the ice into tall glasses of sodas, cocktail mixers. What kind of place deprives babies while using water to garnish drinks?

"I have a policy, Arden. Never back up, always move on. That's what roamers do. It's a luxury, I know." I didn't go into all that it took for me to reach this point, the red tape, the papers and permits I had to file and pay for. People his age didn't even have that option. "But here's what. When we pull over in Griswold, I'll give you an old hockey bag, a big thing that can easily hold four canisters. Hitchhike back to Esterhazy, I mean Potashville, get your family out of there."

"Where should we go? Maybe northwest to BC?"

"You'd have to pass through NUA. Might not get in." Arden looked puzzled. Part of his cluelessness, no doubt, was ignorance. The off-grid dome imposed by many corp-gov towns blocked external information just to keep the population ignorant and subdued. Or subduable.

"Ever since independence, New United Alberta has locked down their borders. Eco-terrorist fears, plus they don't want outsiders nosing around." I'd cut through the country ten days ago with my roamer passport. The old provincial parks still had a few abandoned campgrounds, no amenities but good enough for a few hours' stay. I didn't linger long anywhere, given the gangs of water vultures flitting around in their towering pick-ups with massive wheels. Rock crawlers, they're called, fuelled by gas banned everywhere outside NUA. "Your best bet is north or northeast for the summer." That's about all the advice I could dish out. Pulling into Griswold, autopilot guided us to the recharge station.

Arden opened his harness and went to help me unload the canisters.

"You wait outside." I told him. "It's my bedroom, you know. Off limits." I found the hockey bag, put a few A-Dh lozenges in a side pocket, opened the door and flung the bag onto the pavement. Then I slid four canisters out from under my camper bed and put them by the door. Arden struggled to lift them into the hockey bag. Once it was full, it weighed a ton. He could hardly hoist it. "So drag it," I said. How would he ever get from the highway in Potashville to his house? I'd given up on logic, just wanted him gone.

"You used to play hockey?"

"Nah, but it's a good, sturdy bag." Belonged to Chavez, but I didn't get into that.

By now it was almost nine, and the light was starting to fade. "Go stand under that streetlight on the highway. Someone will pick you up."

My plan was to get some food at the diner next to the recharging station. I plugged the outlet into the camper, Arden's eyes on my back, no doubt hoping I'd change my mind and drive him back to Potashville. "You might as well get going."

"Thanks," he said. "This means a lot." Arden picked up the handles of the hockey bag. Just to give him some courage, I told him about the lozenges in the pocket. He started dragging the bag towards the highway. "Be careful crossing," I yelled. Then, I couldn't resist. I had to ask, "What does Great Forest stand for?"

"My name," he said, turning back for a moment. "Arden means 'great forest.'"

By the time I was installed at my table in the diner, Arden had positioned himself on the highway, thumb out. Standing there in the light of the streetlamp, he looked narrow as a twig. Fragile, too. I was glad to be rid of him, but still, I felt uneasy. Then my food came, real lasagna and a salad with juicy tomatoes, which, after weeks of my dehydrated protein mixes, were overwhelmingly good. I didn't see the vultures come.

When I finished eating, I looked out at the highway. There he lay in the halo of light, a praying mantis face-down in the dirt, the hockey bag nowhere to be seen.

A GREEN AND JUST RECOVERY

Ursula Pflug

Simon cooked rice and vegetables on a green Coleman pump stove. After he'd eaten, he boiled water in his yellow enamel kettle, and then he added tea, a small handful of loose sencha. Later he biked the uphill trails through the woods to the pavilions at the lookout, where there were working outlets. He plugged in his phone and laptop, opened a beer, watched the sunset and chatted with the middle-aged couple at the next table, there doing the same thing. There was only intermittent power in the refitted industrial shed where he lived. Parkview had stayed open because of its resiliency. Chevron had sold it to a small Canadian independent years before, and the refinery had maintained operations. They were the first in British Columbia involved in coprocessing canola and biowaste.

He was still on payroll. There was no rent on the cabin, which the refinery owned, and a little extra showed up in his account every month, enough for tea and beer, his phone, rice, vegetables and secondhand clothes. Mostly he did routine maintenance and the habitat restoration he'd been initially hired for.

Now and then the refinery got hold of a bit of crude via pipeline, and then there were customers who came up the inlet in barges and small product tankers to pick up heating fuel, gasoline or diesel, or even jet fuel. Simon could figure out the different kinds of hookups at the wharf berths. He helped load and kept an extra set of records. And he could talk to people, both the remaining workers and management, as well as the people who came. Some wanted to discuss a delivery of bitumen, not that he was the go-to person for that, or to pick up refined products for transport south. They weren't always involved in strictly legal business, either kind of person, but then it had always been that way, hadn't it? Many of the nations along the pipeline routes from the north and east, including the Secwepemc, maintained their territories were unceded and the pipeline companies had always been trespassers.

> Often I would linger on the way and dream of our life. Was it possible to be so happy? Here we were living on the very windrow of existence, under conditions so poverty stricken and abject in the eyes of the world they were actually condemned in the newspapers, or by the Board of Health, and yet it seemed that we were in heaven and that the world outside—so portentous in its prescriptions for man of imaginary needs that were in reality his damnation—was hell. And for these illusory needs, in that hell of ugliness outside Eridanus, and for the sake of making it a worse hell, men were killing each other. *—Malcolm Lowry*

Nowadays, even if one wanted to live a life of soulless consumption against a backdrop of war and climate chaos, it mostly wasn't possible. All who now saw the poetry in it, could live their own Eridanus. Obviously, Simon's location helped.

Malcolm and Margerie didn't have a child. Their cabin across the water at what was now Cates Park wouldn't have felt as cramped, wouldn't have fallen into disarray so quickly. They were abjectly happy because they hadn't spent enough time yet together to not be.

But they would.

Simon had a set of wooden tiles with paired animals he'd ordered from a Waldorf catalogue for Ben. His ancestry was German, and he couldn't resist. The tiles were for developing memory, but he'd suggested to Hiroko they invent an oracular method for fun.

"We could use the meanings from the David Carson animal cards," she'd said.

"Nah," he'd said. "Let's write our own." Tarot readings were her game. She was good and got paid for it. Their lives crept into one another's. He'd learned from her that, for readings to work, the diviner had to put in a lot of themselves. "If we're going to invent an oracular method," he'd added, "for it to carry any energy, we have to create meanings, not just paste on someone else's."

Hiroko had smiled, hearing herself paraphrased.

He'd always been a scribbler, but it was mostly lists, notes about work and budgets. She was the creative spiritual one, the poet. Still, he'd never lost the habit from the first year of Covid, reading through his notebooks when he was sheltering-in-place. Once when he opened an old journal, he saw she had written: "He is waiting for a story to come in on the tide."

He'd gone outside and looked west, toward the sea. Was a story coming for him, as they had to Lowry? How long did the stories wait to be netted before they drifted away again? Did they breach, like the J pod orcas, so he'd know they were there?

Had Hiroko known something about him he hadn't known about himself?

"There must be some reason you're not supposed to let your spouse do card readings for you," he'd said.

After a long while she'd talked him into it. He hadn't known what to ask. Did she have any suggestions?

"Why am I feeling so stuck in my relationship?"

"Isn't that your question?" he'd asked.

"Is it?"

She had so much edge. He knew she needed it to navigate the world, but he hadn't liked being around it. Maybe he could find the transcribed tarot reading in a notebook. Had the cards told him he'd end up alone, and Hiroko just hadn't mentioned it?

He wanted this. The green stove, the yellow teapot, a few books, his library apps. A beer at the scenic lookout, harmless conversations up there with the couple at the picnic table next to him. The constant negotiating of family life made him crazy. Whose turn was it to make dinner, who was doing childcare tomorrow, who would sweep out the cabin and tidy up their stuff? She'd suggested they make a schedule, but they'd forget to check it and end up with no dinner at all. Uber Eats didn't deliver to the wharves. Ben would get pancakes from a box again, not that he minded.

Their life had been bare bones, but they'd had time and the trails, a view of the water and the water itself, kayaks as well as a runabout. Their beautiful son. Simon knew people who brought him fish, fresh-caught wild salmon when they could get it. Hiroko knew how to slice sashimi correctly and prepared wasabi from scratch. They used to get a couple of cans of Asahi and cook outside on an old Hibachi, high up on the metal framework above the inlet. Ben brought his toys out, big action figures that wouldn't fall through the metalwork to the water far below. Simon and Hiroko had each other. They could make love and cook and talk together. They just hadn't, not much, not in the last year before they left.

At night Simon read. He'd missed it, not having enough time to read. Family life sucked it away.

Simon had Malcolm Lowry's *Hear Us O Lord from Heaven Thy*

Dwelling Place. It was a book Margerie Bonner had put together after Lowry died. He had *Volcano,* of course, much of it written right across the inlet. Simon turned back to Lowry now. He'd read to his son instead of whatever novel he had going. He couldn't blame Ben for taking up his reading time. He loved his son with an abject adoration. There was no one better. Nothing better than being a dad. So many needs Simon hadn't even known he had were answered in the relationship. And he hadn't stopped loving Hiroko, hadn't stopped desiring her. Had they just not managed to structure their lives more positively? They could have each taken a day to themselves when they needed it, a day to air out, walk or bike to Hastings, visit friends, hang out in cafés and bookstores reading and talking. That could have worked.

They could have taken Ben and put more volunteer hours in at the organic farm on the mountain. They didn't get paid except in vegetables. And flowers. Simon loved flowers, especially dahlias and sunflowers. He'd filled the shed with them, and Hiroko had sighed. They couldn't eat flowers. It worked out to less than minimum wage, if he did the math on the trade, but the food from the farm was delicious and healthy, more so than the dented cans at the store. Supply chains were still disrupted; between the pandemic and the wildfires, California's Central Valley agriculture had never fully recovered, either in production or transportation. #EatLocal had never made more sense.

> But could you rent Paradise at twelve dollars a month? was our thought, the next morning, as from the porch of the shack, gazing on the scene of absolute emptiness and solitude, we watched the sunrise bringing the distant power lines across the inlet at Port Boden into relief, the sun sliding up behind the mountain pines, like that blaze behind the pinnacles of a Gothic cathedral, hearing

too, from somewhere, the thrilling diatonic notes of a foghorn in the mist, as if some great symphony had just begun its opening chords.

Twelve dollars a month worked out to well over a hundred now. The shed was free, but Simon worked a few hours every week for Parkview, doing one thing or another. Surely the hut was worth more when there was power? There wasn't a spreadsheet that could integrate all the variables. What was taking Ben out in the canoe at sunrise worth? Mostly the orcas didn't come this far up, but once a whale had waved her flippers in greeting as she passed. Or that was how Ben had described it.

Just and green recovery, their lives had been it.

Hiroko hadn't minded even the winters. Unlike Malcolm and Margerie, they'd had propane and electricity much of the time. Hiroko had lived in tree camps, both the planting kind and the protest kind. She'd been arrested at Fairy Creek, locked in a sleeping dragon the second summer of the pandemic. They hadn't met yet. Simon had worked at the Burnaby terminal that year, while she was up in tripods on the island. When they expanded the tank farm on Burnaby Mountain, they'd hired environmental science grads. He'd helped design mitigation plans for species at risk, including the Sowaqua Spotted Owl, Williamson's Sapsucker and Lewis's Woodpecker.

Simon shook off his nostalgia. Getting lost in the past wouldn't bring her back. And yet there were throughlines, from then till now. Some of the work he did regularly in trade for living in a refurbished industrial shed was still on habitat restoration for the Oregon Spotted Frog, Coastal Giant Salamander and Pacific Water Shrew.

He brought home parts of an old bed he'd bought at the Salvation Army on Hastings. It had lovingly sanded side rails made of high-quality wood. He'd taken them home on his bike and put them up for extra shelves in the shed. He should've done it before Hiroko left. She was always carping about the chaos.

And she would have liked the magic of it. It could be a thrift store, she'd explained, a yard sale, a church sale. Magic, she'd insisted, could flow through the acquisition of meaningful objects at junk stores. An embroidered handkerchief. A set of hand-thrown Japanese bowls. A tiny sweetgrass basket.

"I'm a scientist," he had complained.

"What does it matter? Don't turn down beauty. One day there will be a scientific explanation for it. You can call it magic for now, but you don't have to. Don't turn down beauty."

The wood was so much cheaper than lumber from the yard. The mills had been at reduced capacity for years as so many of the interior roads were impassable in late summer fire season. Plus, there was the history of the beautiful bed rails. Even in the busy Salvation Army, he'd felt the person who had carefully sanded down the boards. That was the kind of thing Hiroko said, the kind of experience she had. Sometimes he'd thought she was poeticizing, confabulating. But in the store, he was convinced he'd truly sensed it, the care and pleasure. If he brought the wood home, he'd have a bit of that joy in his house.

He was a scientist, where was the objective truth in his experience?

Wildfire haze drifted over the inlet. He coughed. He'd been coughing, off and on, for years. It wasn't his few cigarettes.

How magic could flow into your hands, there just for the opening of them, a cloisonné butterfly, a fossil, an embroidered woven handkerchief, things already used by others and made powerful by them. Worn and layered by lives you could lift like smoke, layer after layer, to see the one beneath and the one beneath that, till at last you came clean to the bottom.

He'd found that in a notebook. One of his, not one of hers. Sometimes they wrote a few words or a paragraph in each other's journals. She'd taken hers. Or all the ones she'd found. He might still come across one at the bottom of a box, read it cover to cover, uncover her heart. It had been a rule not to read each other's notebooks, and one they'd both stuck to. It seemed a wonder, that, considering all the other vows they'd broken.

Don't be ungrateful.

She'd written it, though, in the same yellow foolscap pad where he'd found: "He is waiting for a story to come in on the tide."

Funny he should find it today.

He kept books in piles. The new shelves would help with that. There were more out again, as he'd gone back to uncrating journals after Hiroko and Ben left. Her leaving had reminded him of quarantine, now long ago. Just when he could ramble more without neglecting his domestic duties, he'd instead huddled alone in the shed. Maybe what he'd wanted was not to get out more but to have the place to himself, see the world in a grain of sand.

He had Lao Tzu's *Tao Te Ching*, Ursula LeGuin's translation.

47 Looking Far

You don't have to go out the door
To know what goes on in the world.

You don't have to look out the window
To see the way of heaven.
The farther you go,
The less you know.

So the wise soul
Doesn't go, but knows;
Doesn't look, but sees;
Doesn't do, but gets it done.

Leafing through foolscap pads, Simon saw he'd written more poetry than he thought. And dreams.

In the afternoon the pale light.
The Vancouver summer wanes.
In two days it will be September. A sweet tiredness.
The sweet tiredness of the young,
feeling old before they are old.

Walking with you in the streets, hand in hand.
This our lives.
This our youth.
These very days that are passing now.
On the verge of our lives.
In the afternoon the pale light.

On the verge of their lives indeed. It was a few months before she'd gotten pregnant.

Sometimes at night he had thrown the coins, long before Hiroko. She was the professional diviner, but he'd consulted the *I-Ching* since his teens. He had a degree in environmental science and filled the cabin with flowers for the aesthetics while she traded the Latin names of *brassicaceae* with the organic farmers on the mountain.

They kept a few in boxes outside on the platform, sturdy cultivars that could manage the wind that sometimes blasted down from the mountains or from the sea.

Mizuna and rabe had been their favourites, and even Ben had come to love them.

Brassica juncea var. *japonica.*

Brassica rapa var. *Ruvo.*

He could see the brilliant-yellow mustard flowers through the big window Parkview had let him put in. Bees sometimes came up all this way to gather pollen.

Simon couldn't find the book, sorting through the stacks on the floor around his bed. He'd wanted to put it on his new shelves, with the journals he was currently reading. He could keep the animal tiles on the new shelves too, and a few printouts of pictures of Hiroko and Ben. Shells and stones and feathers. He kept looking. Hiroko might have taken it, thinking it was hers. After all, she could have used it for work. She understood modalities from a broad range of cultures.

The next time he was recharging at the pavilion at sunset, he looked it up. He tried not to use his phone as a hotspot at home, burn through data. He wanted the edition he'd lost track of, the hardcover Wilhelm/Baynes, with its distinctive grey and yellow cover. It was too expensive. He'd have to take the bus to Kits, to Banyen Books, to see if they had a used copy.

He should write while he was here. If he wrote loosely, without forethought, more stream-of-consciousness prose poetry than a planned attack, themes and images might emerge. The story might come in on the tide. He'd brought the yellow pad, abandoned years ago when it was still mostly empty. He could have written on his charging laptop, but handwriting accessed a different part of his brain, one he wanted now.

He wrote not the beginning of a story but a dream from the night before: "I proceed to put butter and jam on the pages of this notebook where there is nothing written, and eat them, wondering vaguely if I have forgotten to check whether there is writing on the other side."

Maybe he wasn't eating enough. Maybe Hiroko had cooked more than he'd thought.

He worked out his finances for the rest of the week. He had $100.00 for groceries and sundries till the first of the month. He could buy a second hand *I-Ching* at Banyen Books if he biked across town instead of taking a crowded bus. It was safer, not just cheaper. The coronavirus always came back with the colder weather. Hardly anyone died anymore, but it was nasty enough to be worth avoiding. Most people wore masks in winter, as much to deflect colds and flu as Covid. And in fire season they protected against particulate inhalation.

Simon wanted the Wilhelm/Baynes badly. He didn't have many books. Most of them had been Hiroko's. Or Ben's. He didn't need Wi-Fi to read digital library books, but he missed print, missed the heft and the smell. Older books were better for that. And the *I-Ching* didn't exist on library apps.

His life plan for the week depressed him. The shed without Hiroko and Ben felt paltry. Malcolm wrote *Under the Volcano* with years of Margerie's concerted editorial input. There is a story coming in on the tide, we better go fish for it. They had done a good job, fishing together for what some called the last great modernist novel.

Idly, he looked up *I-Ching* sites. Fishing coins from his pocket, he stilled his mind before throwing them. The hexagram would be the correct one.

Hexagram: 37

Name: Chia Jen.

Keyphrase: The family.

Formed By The Trigrams: Wind over Fire.

General: Open and respectful communication is the key to making a team work successfully.

Love: Communication must be sincere to benefit your relationship.

It wasn't the Wilhelm/Baynes but a random *I-Ching* site. He didn't read the entire entry, but still he could see Hiroko, in a faded yellow cotton T-shirt, her long dark hair pulling loose from a ponytail. Motherhood sucked the life right out of a woman. Not that he cared about the old T-shirts. Hiroko was beautiful. She was at home in her body, and that lent her a grace and confidence that clothes or heels or makeup never could. Besides, women who dressed to the nines when their children were infants had to be letting them scream while they preened in front of the mirror.

Simon had never made the animal tiles oracle, but it might be time to begin. He had oil lamps at the shed and could work late into the evening even if the power cut out, writing down possible meanings and working out methods of divination. He'd write the meanings in the old yellow foolscap pad. It was bringing him luck.

He shuffled the tiles, asking, How do I escape if the wildfires come to my house?

He drew three tiles and set them in a row.

Frog. Goose. Wombat.

The Leopard Frog knows how to hop over obstacles to reach the water.

The Canada Goose mates for life.

The Wombat shared its tunnels with echidnas and wallabies during the worst of the Australian burning.

Simon wrote the meanings down carefully. Maybe this was his story. It wasn't tarot or the *I-Ching*, but it could be, after a few hundred years of tweaking.

—

Excerpts from "The Forest Path to the Spring," by Malcolm Lowry from *MacLean's* Magazine, July 15, 1961.

Lao-Tzu: Tao Te Ching: A Book about the Way and the Power of the Way by Ursula K. LeGuin. Shambhala, October 20, 1998.

GREY-ISH

Ian Thomas Shaw

The last gas station in Canada closed last week. It had long been reserved exclusively for old-timers—the ancient gas-guzzlers that so many of us had hung on to out of nostalgia. I plead guilty as charged for still driving one of them—a 1997 Mercedes C230 sedan. It was a beautiful beast and had a good half-century run. I watch from my living room as my Merc is hitched up by the tow woman. My neighbours also gather to watch the spectacle. A little girl, about five years old, spots me looking through the window and waves. Her older brother gives me the thumbs-down, as if I'm next. Fat chance, kid. I'm no gas-guzzler, and flatulence hasn't been criminalized yet.

As you can guess, I'm an elderly gent, mostly bionic with a lot of Costco aftermarket parts. But I'm still ticking and not ready to cryptocurrency it in yet. My AI implant reminds me to keep walking —500 steps per hour—or risk an electric shock. I curse my nephew, the neuro-app designer, for insisting on implanting this device. I had been doing fine without it, keeping in shape by tending my garden. Then the environmental police showed up. They informed me that ornamental flowers and shrubs had been banned, and my yard would be confiscated for community gardening. I offered to grow the vegetables myself, but they refused, saying all volunteer positions had been taken by underrepresented communities and environmental refugees. As compensation, they offered increased food rations: two extra litres of kombucha and ten kilos of kale per month. I reluctantly accepted, since they threatened to cancel my government pension if I did not comply. My meagre savings in my secret Bitcoin account in the Federal Union of China, Korea and Russia (FUCKR) wouldn't be enough to live on. Sometimes, I thought about immigrating to FUCKR. They still have gas there, and I had heard good things about Supreme Leader Vlad-Xi Putin-Jining, the test tube offspring of the founding fathers.

I tap my forehead twice to activate the entertainment centre implant in my frontal cortex. After ten minutes of government-sanctioned news, mostly optimistic projections about the production of "environmentally appropriate" crops, I manage to tune in to the debates in the House of Commons. They're discussing how to deal with the influx of refugees from what used to be Central America. Rising sea levels have turned it into a bunch of islands. The nation of Panama is totally gone. As water poured in from both the Pacific and the Atlantic, the width of the canal went from 300 metres to 300 kilometres. The Americans, FUCKRians and WTO aren't complaining. Now their kilometre-wide container ships and egos can pass through unimpeded and fee-free. Another win for global trade!

Elizabeth May still leads the Evergreen Party and is now Prime Minister, though that doesn't mean much. After the interminable Trudeau government declared bankruptcy thanks to Canada's IMF debts and arrears in paying NATO assessments of fifty percent of GDP, UN auditors were put in charge of liquidating our national assets. Liberal and Conservative politicos promptly cashed in their Bitcoin stock options in Meta and Google and headed to Cuba for cheap health care, leaving the Evergreens as the last political party in the country. As ex-Prime Minister Justin Trudeau boarded his jet for the Aga Khan's Caribbean resort, he proudly brainwaved, "I've made reconciliation possible. Good luck with the rest!" Indigenous people across the country's moonscape surface bid the Great White Father goodbye with single-digit waves.

The UN auditors tried to auction off most of the country to international consortia, but buyers weren't exactly lining up, except for the vintage Céline Dion LPs, snapped up by Supreme Leader Vlad-Xi Putin-Jinping. Most of the scorched, soggy and totally uninhabitable moonscapes of Canada were returned to the indigenous communities, as per Justin's last executive order. "Guard them well!" he blathered as they looked on in dismay at the burnt tree trunks, dried up peat moss and tornado-etched craters. Later, the now ice-free, underwater Nunavut was sold off to Greenpeace as a preserve for the surviving narwhals and a smack of foot-field-long jellyfish.

The ever-acquisitive Elon Musk bought Kingston, home of his alma mater Queen's University, and turned it into a mega-museum of his accomplishments. The city's skyline now features a two-kilometre-high, pink projectile with a small fountain on top, named appropriately *Elonia.*

The rights to Quebec were largely sold to a maple syrup consortium headquartered in Montreal and led by none other than Donald Trump, as svelte as he ever was and still looking youthful and orange thanks to AI skin technology. As soon as the deal was completed, Trump rushed to the ramparts of Quebec City and thundered, "Make Maple Syrup Great Again!" Politicians from the governing Coalition pour l'Avenir du Québec now occupy seats on the consortium's board, proudly wearing their red MMSGA caps. The consortium even struck a deal with the opposition Parti Québécois, providing them with Teslas festooned with Quebec flags.

Ottawa, with its sidekick city of Gatineau, has become the "Venice of the North." After the floods of 2030, most of the city was underwater, although the deluge did have a silver lining: it saved the capital from burning to the ground when raging wildfires engulfed the Gatineau Park. Prime Minister Trudeau, with his characteristic flourish and rare foresight, purchased the entire gondola fleet of the real Venice, the Italian city long since returned to the Adriatic. Since then, Ottawa tourism has flourished, with Chinese visitors taking underwater photos of the former By market and kayaking around the half-submerged Peace Tower.

Not all of Canada went under the gavel, though. Vancouver Island, with its monopoly on organic garlic fertilized by orca poop, and PEI, profiting from the franchising of Anne of Green Gables houses in Asia, managed to remain financially solvent and escape UN tutelage. Elizabeth May then used a grant from the World Wildlife Federation to bribe them to join her in a new confederation. However, the WWF grant required that the country be renamed the Wildlife Trust Fund of Canada. Thus, WTF Canada was born.

Since massive forests, forest fires, and overzealous organic garlic farming had wiped out most of the wildlife in WTF Canada, May imported an adorable pair of capybaras from the remaining ten square kilometres of the Brazilian rainforest. In no time, the nation's canals were teeming with these randy critters, pushing out the lowly beavers. The new WTF Canada flag proudly displays this new national symbol, the world's largest water rat. May also solved unemployment, hunger, obesity and the patriarchy in one fell swoop by offering every citizen guaranteed minimum rations of kombucha and kale for life, financed by indenturing all men under eighty to serve in UN peacekeeping operations and lending a few to the Wagner Group for extra cash.

I miss the old country. But I am an aging white man, and, as a friend in Montreal keeps reminding me, “It’s time to move on.” She even includes an application for MAID with her latest brain-mail. And no, MAID isn’t a “maid,” though I could use one of those. It stands for “Medical Assistance In Dying,” another legacy program of our island-hopping former Prime Minister. I quickly forwarded the application to Justin’s last known address with the words, “Thanks for reconciliation, and good luck with this!” My friend has also attached her fifty-fifth draft of a novel for me to comment on. Thanks to JammerGPT, I respond within seconds with insightful comments: “Creative, Reflective, Absorbing and Promising.” I get a yayayaya for my efforts and a coupon for a virtual reality sex doll with interchangeable genitalia. Familiarity breeds contempt, I sigh, and redeem the coupon.

I won’t be visiting Montreal anytime soon. The MMSGA Corporation requires a building pass to enter ninety percent of the former province, which is now their private property, and residents of WTF Canada are considered a health risk due to the 999th variant of Covid. Apparently, it was spread by capybara turds on the local kale crop. The building pass was board member and former premier François Legault’s idea.

I had considered taking my old Mercedes on its last tank of gas and heading for Montreal to see my friend, but with military drones darkening the border skies, it wasn’t worth the risk. Besides, my friend isn’t much fun anymore; she’s been constipated for a quarter-century and spends eighty percent of her time on the toilet writing novels. However, she does enjoy the good life, consuming copious amounts of contraband chocolate, Korean BBQ and chardonnay, which probably explains the constipation. Money is no object. As part of the takeover agreement, the MMSGA consortium guaranteed perpetual, very generous cultural grants to professional writers and the purchase of all copies of their e-books for the board's private collection (paper was banned in 2030 to save the environment). It was the perfect solution for social harmony. Writers could write as many subversive, Creative, Reflective, Absorbing and Promising books as they wanted, and the innocent minds of the populace would be protected from them, allowing workers to focus on Making Maple Syrup Great Again!

I look outside. The Merc is gone, and the sky is grey. I've met my walking quota for now and avoided electrocution for at least another hour. In the community garden that was my yard, a group of hungry environmental refugees from Panama toil away, weeding under the watchful eye of the garden's security cameras. In a blind spot, one of the workers sets an illegal trap for capybaras and the occasional mutant squirrel—both tasty barbecue treats. I venture onto my backyard deck, which sways and creaks—or maybe it's just my knees. The cedars are all dead now, and my white ash is leafless. The refugees have removed the pavers I once meticulously laid to create a French country garden and have used them to build makeshift shelters in the waterlogged parking lots of dilapidated shopping centres. In the areas of the garden not reserved for kale production, pale, drab weeds have taken over. Not the vibrant green weeds we once knew, the ones my friend once encouraged me to let grow for the sake of the environment. Now I wish I had.

Sometimes I think about writing a novel about how things could have been, a nice comforting fiction where a new generation, one that hasn't come out of a test tube, challenges the status quo and finds a sustainable balance between progress and preservation. Or maybe not. Like my fossil-fueled Merc, I feel like a fossil myself—a relic of a bygone era. The world around me has turned to shades of grey, both figuratively and literally.

With a sigh, I delete my virtual reality sex doll from my frontal cortex entertainment centre. There are more important things to focus on than temporal pleasures. It's time to rise to the challenge, to fight for a greener future. And maybe, just maybe, I can leave my mark on this new WTF Canada and bequeath a legacy that future generations will remember—one of hope, humour and environmental stewardship. My ego swells, almost as large as the Elonia monument. Then I calm down and watch capybaras playfully frolic in a nearby canal of our Venice of the North. Maybe I will put off this new chapter of my life. It does sound strenuous. Things will eventually sort themselves out. They always do. And anyway, I have lots of time. Why rush? I'm only ninety-two.

ANTHOLOGY CONTRIBUTORS

Sang Kim

Born in South Korea, Sang is a writer and celebrity chef who lives in Toronto. He is the winner of the Gloria Vanderbilt/ Exile Editions Short Fiction Prize for his short story "When John Lennon Died" in the *CVC: Carter V. Cooper Short Fiction Anthology Series. Book Six.* His short fiction has appeared in many Canadian literary magazines and in *The Marginal Ride Anthology* (Deux Voiliers Publishing). He is also a playwright: *Ballad of a Karaoke Cowboy* (Variety Crossing Press) and *A Dream Called Laundry* (KCLF-21 Publication). His TV show, "Searching with Chef Sang", premiered in September 2023, on TLN.

Jerry Levy

Originally from Montreal, Jerry now resides in Toronto, Ontario, and works in the corporate world. He has published over twenty-five stories in various literary magazines and anthologies. In the fall of 2013, a collection of fourteen stories, *Urban Legend*, was published by Thistledown Press. His second collection of short stories, *The Quantum Theory of Love and Madness*, was published by Guernica Editions in 2020. His third collection, *The Philosopher Stories*, was published by Guernica in 2024. He was also a contributor to *The Marginal Ride Anthology* (Deux Voiliers Publishing).

Michael Mirolla

The author of a clutch of novels, short story and poetry collections, plays, and film scripts, Michael's publications include a novella, *The Last News Vendor*, winner of the 2020 Hamilton Literary Award for fiction, as well as three Bressani Prizes: the novel *Berlin* (2010); the poetry collection *The House on 14th Avenue* (2014); and the short story collection *Lessons in Relationship Dyads* (2016). His poetry collection, *At the End of the World*, was short-listed for the 2022 Hamilton Literary Award. A symposium on Michael's writing was held in Toronto on May 25, 2023. He was also a contributor to *The Marginal Ride Anthology* (Deux Voiliers Publishing). Born in Italy and raised in Montreal, Michael now lives in Hamilton.

Matthew Murphy

Matt was born and raised in Sudbury, Ontario. He currently lives in Montreal, where he works as a writer and a teacher. He is the author of *A Beckoning War* (Baraka Books, 2016) and is currently seeking publication for his second novel, *Fugitive Dreams*.

Tim Niedermann

A native New Englander by birth, Tim divides his time between Bethany, Connecticut and Montreal. He is both a contributor and co-editor of the *Green to Grey* anthology. He is the author of the novel *Wall of Dust* (Deux Voiliers Publishing), set in the Occupied Palestinian Territories. He was a contributor and was the co-editor of *The Marginal Ride Anthology* (Deux Voiliers Publishing). Tim has been a professional editor for most of his career dealing with subject matter ranging from sports to law to public policy to celebrity biography. He is a regular reviewer for the *Ottawa Review of Books*.

Ursula Pflug

Born in Tunis to German parents in 1958, Ursula grew up in Toronto and currently lives in the village of Norwood, near Peterborough,

Ontario. She has published three novels: *Motion Sickness* (Inanna Publications), *The Alphabet Stones* (Blue Denim Press) and *Green Music* (Tesseract Books). She has also published two short story collections: *Harvesting the Moon* (PS Publishing) and *After the Fires* (Tightrope Book). She also contributed two stories to the *Marginal Ride Anthology* (Deux Voiliers Publishing).

Ian Thomas Shaw

Ian was born in Vancouver, British Columbia. He has published two novels, *Quill of the Dove* (Guernica Editions) and *Soldier, Lily, Peace and Pearls* (Deux Voiliers Publishing), translated Andrée A. Gratton's *Choisir Éléonore* into English (*Choosing Eleonore,* Guernica Editions) and translated into French *Quill of the Dove* (*La colombe,* Éditions David). He co-edited and contributed two stories to *The Marginal Ride Anthology* (Deux Voiliers Publishing). For more than thirty years, he worked as a diplomat and as an international development worker, living in Africa, the Middle East and Europe. He currently lives in Aylmer, Quebec. He is the founder of Deux Voiliers Publishing, the Prose in the Park Literary Festival and the Ottawa Review of Books.

Cora Siré

Cora lives in Montréal and is the author of a collection of short stories, *Fear the Mirror* (Véhicule Press), two novels, *Behold Things Beautiful* (Signature Editions) and *The Other Oscar* (Quattro Books) and two poetry collections, *Not In Vain You've Sent Me Light* (Guernica Editions) and *Signs of Subversive Innocents* (Signature Editions). Her work has appeared in magazines and anthologies in

Canada, the US, Mexico and Europe. She is also the co-creator of the short film *I Want More Life to Love!*

Caroline Vu

Born in Vietnam, Caroline lives in Montreal. She was the recipient of the Canadian Authors Association's Fred Kerner Award for her first novel *Palawan Story* (Deux Voiliers Publishing) and has since written two more novels: *That Summer in Provincetown* (Guernica Editions) and *Catinat Boulevard* (Guernica Editions). All of her novels have been translated into French and published by Éditions de la Pleine Lune. She also contributed two stories to *The Marginal Ride Anthology* (Deux Voiliers Publishing).

MIX
Paper
FSC® C100212

Printed by Imprimerie Gauvin
Gatineau, Québec